A Rainbow After the Storm

Book One

Of

The Storm Tales

by

G. W. "Tabbi" Duggan

A Rainbow after the Storm

Copyright © 2014 by G. W. Duggan

ISBN: 978-1-62217-442-3

This is a story of growth and empowerment. It's about overcoming obstacles that become the tools that shape and transform lives as well as allowing one's experiences, to strengthen and act as a guide throughout this continually changing journey called life.

The Stephens family; in actuality are a group of people connected by biology, but with no emotional ties and very little knowledge about each other. Individually, they are meant to assist in the readers self-evaluation while reflecting, parts of us that some people would wish to remain hidden and unknown.

We encounter a man incapable of loving anything or anyone. He feels justified and correct in his abusive behavior, when in truth, his insecurities cause his violent attacks on those around him when unsure of how to express his pain.

We identify a woman on the verge of change. A change so dramatic that it's force alters everything around her like a tsunami. A violent evolution from the passive, docile young woman into a vengeful and murderous wife that refuses to accept that her marriage is not the fairytale she believed it to be.

We watch a youth, caged by strong emotions that are not tempered by the size of a perceived enemy. The threat to what you hold dear acts as the opening of a spillway on a son's protective instincts, fuel for flames of hatred, contained by his love for those he feels he must protect at any cost.

We embrace unprotected innocence, that continually left unguarded, will eventually meet with a fate worse than death. A shattering of something so fragile it will take a lifetime to heal the pain and turmoil of a multitude of sins performed against it.

This is the story of one family›s attempt to recover from living beneath skies full of clouds that bring about the storms of rage, which have left them tattered and torn. They must all learn that some skies hold beautiful colors forming the rainbow of happiness, appreciated most by those who've weathered the storm.

Reviews

"This powerful woman of grace, class and dignity; has managed to capture the epitome of Shakespeare's, "To thine own self be true."
~ L. Y. White

"It is a rare event to witness the human spirit triumph over such adversity and become an inspiration to others. But through positivism, humor and deep faith G. W. Duggan has created a work that will shock you, make you cry, make you laugh and affect you in ways you never thought possible. It is a blessing to be able to be a part of this wonderful woman's' journey."
~L. Baker

"I feel that this book will touch the wounded parts of all of us who wear masks of joy, happiness and contentment when deep, deep down inside we carry a story similar to Ms. Duggan's characters. You feel that this book is describing You and many events we have all experienced but would not know where to start expressing the ghastly and vast hurt some of these character's (and us) go through. Ms. Duggan hits the nail right on the head."
~X. Jones

Dedication

This book is dedicated to those three important persons affected by domestic violence:

The abused-So you know that your experiences do not define you, but contribute to the unique individual you inevitably become.

The abuser-The goal is to eradicate the acceptance of domestic violence and disavow the common belief that it is only the physical contact that hurts.

The witnesses-So you become aware and recognize the lasting often permanent effects of all types of violence, and make it impossible for you to remain silent to the suffering of others. To educate everyone to the experiences of the abused, because education and enlightenment is just as significant to healing as treating the physical wounds.

This book is dedicated to all those that have suffered at the feet of the parasitic disease known as domestic violence. For no one infected or affected by this disease, for surely it can be called nothing else, will be the same once it is removed. So please think before you act, and be aware of those innocent eyes watching, learning and being forever altered by violence, its presence, its existence and its healing.

Foreword

Pain, shame, isolation, and fear. These are just a few emotions that many among us live with on a day to day basis. For many, this is the sum-total of their existence. From abused and molested children who live in fear and victimization of those who are supposed to look out for and protect them. To adults who live with emotional and physical abuse at the hands and tongues of those they have given their hearts to. Pain, shame, isolation and fear. These and other negative emotions have caused many to give up on life, love and living.

Yet, there are some who, not only live through the pain, shame and fear, but who grow from it. There are some who use these negative feelings and experiences to push them to seek something better for themselves and those around them. There are those who not only survive, but are determined to thrive in spite of the pain. DeTalia Stephens is one such person.

In spite of the very destructive things that has taken place in her life, in spite of the pain, DeTalia Stephens has decided to use her experiences to encourage herself and others who live through what she lived through and similar experiences to seek the "Rainbow after the Storm."

This book is a work that will inform and empower all who read it. Even if you have not lived through the various destructive experiences Dee and others have lived through, at times we all encounter painful, fearful experiences. Her openness, honesty and the brave way she confronts the demons of her past is a lesson to us all that, we too, can find our 'rainbow after the storm."

Thank you DeTalia. Thank you for not hiding your past hurt. Thank you for putting the abuse and fear that many families live with on "front Street" for all to see, by allowing G.W. Duggan to tell your story. You have shown us that we cannot bury our heads in the sand as if these things do not and are not taking place. Many right next door to where we live, in our churches, schools and social circles. Thank you for having the courage to share your story and turning your mess into a message. Thank you for letting us all know, that if we search hard enough and hold on, we too will find A RAINBOW AFTER THE STORM.

God bless you.
Dr. Gregory M. Fuller

The characters found here are not real people,
nor are the events that take place.

Any characters or events that may resemble real
situations &/or persons, are purely coincidental.

Contents

PROLOGUE.....

Let me begin.....

Life has taught me many things, some of them have caused unrealistic fears to take root and others to make me aggressive when patience would do. The one most important lesson is that everyone has a story. Some happy, some sad and some simply horrific and scarring; but in a world such as this there are a plethora of stories. Because I have learned that some stories can heal simply in the telling, some in the hearing and others because the shaping of a life has occurred in such a way that the story must be told; this is such a story. For those that share the experiences of this particular group, know that life can often take you places you never wished to go.

As the mother of four children, Joshua, 14; Brandon, 11; Nikol, 10; and Gregory, 7; my goal has been to raise my children with as much of a normal childhood as possible. But then we all have various definitions of normal. Let's just say that my children will hopefully never know a childhood such as the one my brother and I shared.

I was born DeTalia Yvonne Stephens, but everyone calls me Dee. My mother gave me this nickname for two reasons; mostly because my father did not like the name and also because most people cannot pronounce it correctly. I have one sibling, Skylur Carrington Stephens, two years my senior. My brother is called Sky because I have always and still do, look up to him.

My brother and I were mentally and emotionally scarred by our childhood, with my brother being physically abused as well. We grew up in a house that entertained very little peace and quiet. Understanding never dwelled let alone came to visit our house and would not have received a warm welcome if it stopped by. It will forever be remembered as a house, never a home, because it was a place where we simply existed.

Sky, for reasons few really know, remains single and mostly alone. My brother felt that if our father could behave in the manner in which he did, while proclaiming boundless love for his family, he did not want any affiliation with the institute of marriage, nor any children that would be a product of it.

Sky told me many times during our younger years; he felt his rage and hatred, for our treatment, would be contained only because he was unable to express it fully, due to his youth. His fear was that should he allow himself to fall in love his inner demons would somehow find their way out and shatter any hopes of his having a "normal" family life. Thereby, making him a clone of our father. The one thing he least wanted to be or resemble in any way.

There is no point in time that I can remember where my parents' marriage changed from being happy to the almost daily hell it had become. Maybe it was never happy, but at some point around my turning 7 or 8 things changed drastically. What catalyst brought about the change, who can say but I do know that around this time what Sky and I thought were arguments and fights on television turned out to be fights between our parents.

It was at this time that they no longer tried to mask the sounds with the radio or television turned up loud. Or maybe they were just louder than the TV or radio. Needless to say we became aware of the fighting, we also became aware that our mother was not as clumsy as our father had previously lead us to believe. The frequent black eyes and other bruises were not caused by falls, at least not falls from mother's own "clumsiness".

Then began the constant screaming and fighting in our house. Many trips to St. Michael's Hospital and numerous nights spent at someone's house to prevent us from seeing what we already knew was happening. Adults never understand that simply because a child does not see it or hear it, does not mean that children don't know about it, or that it won't have a lasting impression. It would be surprising to most, but then; maybe it wouldn't.

Our father, Jonathan Stephens, had much hatred pent up inside. He projected the image of a maniacal person. Whose only form of self-expression was rage and violence. He appeared to be afraid of his feelings.

Feelings for everyone, especially my mother. He would beat her when he made mistakes or when life did not go as he wished.

His image seemed to be what mattered most to him. He had to be known as the man with the best of everything. And if things were not that way it was my mother's fault and he let her know it, in no uncertain terms. He would take no responsibility for the unfinished, the incomplete, or the incorrect. None of these occurred, in our house, through any fault of his; or so he behaved.

My brother must have felt the need to protect our mother. Because he began to insinuate himself into the arguments between my parents. Which lead to him being beaten as well. For whatever unknown reason, my father saw fit to spare me. Maybe it was okay to be known for abusing your wife but not your daughter. I understand this no better today than I did as a child and I see no difference now nor did I then.

My mother, Maria, suffered mental and physical cruelty at the hands of a man incapable of love and intimacy. After many years of abuse and mental torture she struck back, at life and at my father, in the most vengeful way she knew how. The way my father taught her, through anger and violence....

CHAPTER ONE.....
THE DIARY

For more than four years, probably many more, my mother was being severely and constantly abused by my father. Why it continued as long as it did I have no idea. But I know that at some point my mother became tired. Tired of the abuse and maybe tired of my father.

One day I came in the kitchen and mother was standing at the sink staring out the window. She did not seem to notice I was there, not even when I spoke to her. Sky came in and spoke to her and got the same response as I, none. Then she started talking, not really to us and not really to anyone; just talking. She said enough was enough, and she had had enough. It was time for a change. At this point she turned and looked at us sitting at the table and we saw someone we had never seen before. No not a stranger, but another side of our mother. If rebellion had a visage and a voice, then it was surely standing in our kitchen that day.

This was a day like many others, it was a morning following a night of arguing and fighting. This was apparent by the broken dishes and small splatters of blood I noticed here and there in the living room as I passed thru on my way to the kitchen.

My mother never saw fit to explain to us why we lived in the manner in which we did, the constant fights, bloody arguments and constant washing of walls and painting. But this day she said that there would be an ending to finding herself on the floor in a battered and bloody heap. Mother said there was fast approaching an ending to waking up with eyes swollen shut and lips so bruised and sore it would be days before she could eat normally. Mother said she wanted a life where she held her children and not them holding her in a puddle of blood on the floor.

No more having her children perfect the skill of painting walls before they could learn to color inside the lines in a coloring book.

This Maria we did not know, my mother never spoke this way not even when my father was not at home. Mother always carried herself and spoke as if father could hear her every word maybe even hear her thoughts as well. Somehow the most recent episode, as we had begun calling them, had not only broken all the dishes in the dining room, but something inside mother as well.

This is the point where I remember things actually beginning to change. Little things that I was too young to notice but, felt the shift in the atmosphere of our house. Just walking through the rooms felt like I was in another house different from the one where I had lived all my eight years. It is at this point that I will tell the details of our lives. The story of how we, Sky and I became the individuals that you will come to know. It is this point where my mothers' rebellion began, therefore, it is truly the beginning.

Mother began her rebellion in a slow and insidious manner that climaxed with an eruption of events that would forever change the lives of everyone in our house. As memory serves me well it was in the spring of the year that I realized that things were no longer as they had always been. My mother always did exactly as my father said, if he did not like something it was not allowed in the house or disappeared very quickly. My mother never had a rebellious nature nor was she one for instigating situations of discord, but the woman I knew as mother was about to take a permanent vacation and leave behind an individual that cared very little about how things were, but focused only on how they would change and drastically.

To insinuate the change that would be cataclysmic, my mother began keeping a diary. A simple thing one might say, but for mother it was the beginning of an end.

Many times my mother would mention starting a diary and my father would berate and belittle her. He would refer to her as having a level of stupidity that was beyond him. He said simpleminded people who could not maintain a thought for more than a few moments kept diaries. People that had nothing better to do but scribble down page after page of nonsense that no one was interested in, so they wasted paper and killed trees uselessly to keep collections of their ramblings. So in keeping with her norm mother always abandoned the idea. But this time was to be different. She did not announce her decision but instead, just began writing daily in secret and keeping it hidden.

There were times when we would find mother quiet and alone just writing, neither Sky nor I asked what she was doing or what she was writing. I think we both suspected it was a diary or a journal of some sort but by not saying it out loud or asking the question and having it confirmed we claim ignorance and avoided father's anger if questioned.

Truth be told, mother no longer cared if father found out about the writings, she no longer cared if he agreed or disagreed with her wishes. I think that mother had changed so drastically that she wanted him to know her feeling and would soon make them known with or without the diary.

Who knew that during the day when she was home alone and needing to fill endless lonely hours she would write. She would sit and write as a form of release. She wrote about the things that made her happy and that distressed her. She had started by writing about her disappointment with her marriage and the person that my father had become. She wrote of her love for us, her children, and her prayers that we would grow to be all that she and my father were not. She wrote of her friends for which we knew her to have only a chosen few; writing about their outings that were never known about or discussed. She wrote about the loss of one of her greatest passions, art. Her lost dreams of decorating and creating beautiful homes for people to not just entertain in and show off; but homes real homes where real people lived, loved and raised their children. Places that people couldn't wait to get back to at the end of a long day and just enjoyed being there because it was comfortable and it was theirs. She wrote about the life she would have had if her husband had been the man he pretended to be or the man she believed him to be.

She progressed with her daily ritual of writing in her journal until she became comfortable with the idea; and comfortable that he, my father, and his thoughts were no longer an issue. No longer was she fearful of him becoming aware of her secret. Neither did she care what his reactions would be, if he discovered her defiance of his feelings.

Once she had been writing and she left her diary lying on the table. My brother and I found it. It was then that we became aware of the diary and learned the truth about our parents and their marriage. Thus, I am now able to relay the account of events that changed the lives of a group of people living together and calling themselves a family, which the emotional connections that existed in our house were more or less the equivalent of wet paper.

My brother and I read those pages, with much regret for having done so. Our regret was not so much for reading the diary, but that we shared parts of our mother's wish. Especially my brother. Regret because there was no longer a curtain of lies to hide the truth of how little my parents cared for each other. Which to me translated as a lack of love for us as well. Because if their love for each other was not real then how could their love for us be.

My mother did not show the restraint in her writing that she had often shown in her daily existence. She spoke of the times when things were different, when she honestly believed that our father loved her or at least held some fondness for her. Her writings talked about the early years of their marriage when father came home at night glad to see her. The times when he would hold her and reassure her. Then, Sky and I started to appear in her writings as well as father's change in attitude and treatment of her. How for years she had lived with the abuse, the other women, and the lack of compassion was of less concern than his abuse of her and her feelings. This went on for many pages as Sky read aloud the awful things that had been occurring for years, which we had no idea was happening.

Mother wrote what she would want her life to be like instead of what we were actually living. How she had wanted to complete her college degree and use her talents to create paintings and to decorate beautiful homes including her own. Instead she spent days and nights hiding in her house so no one saw the full extent of her injuries and bruises. So none of her friends would know that her own husband had taken from her one of her greatest passions by breaking her wrist and several of her fingers in one his rages. Now painting was no longer an option or even a possibility, actually she could barely write and at times even that was painful.

Then, her writings took on another tone altogether. Her writings became angrier and more dangerous, carrying within it the equivalent of a deep roar. Something akin to an evil heavy presence lurking just there behind you in the dark. Something so sinister that even the stoutest of heart would fear its steady approach. One might even say, her words became a death toll. She started writing about her true feelings. Expressing the desire to see my father experience the pain and torture she had endured for the last few years. She wrote about her pain and anger, just as she had written of her dreams. She wrote of new dreams and wishes. Her greatest wish was my father's fatal demise. She had drawn a very vivid image of the things she wished to come to pass for our father. She wanted him to experience the pain she was feeling, caused by having the one thing you love most become the catalyst for your undoing. For her, it was him; in his case it would be his beloved Harley-Davidson.

She wrote about how satisfactory it would be to have him have a blowout on his motorcycle; hoping it would leave him paralyzed. She wanted him to be completely helpless, the way she had felt the last few years of their marriage. This made my brother fear for my mother, if father ever found her diary; it made me fear for my father because in spite of what he was I still loved him.

We all suffered because of the diary. Initially my brother and I. Later my mother would, because it was what she wanted for him and she may have spoken her own undoing. Later it would be said that father knew about the diary and had maybe even read some of it and that would be the explanation for his actions. This was not mother's intent and then, maybe it was. But in her tormented mind and battered body, it was an attempt to express her refusal to allow this treatment to continue.

CHAPTER TWO.....
THE SHOOTINGS

So begins a chapter of my life, which I shall never forget, and an ending to many chapters of suffering. An ending for my brother, because he could never stand by and watch. Subjecting himself to the abuse intended for my mother, hoping that would be enough for father and maybe he would grant mother a night of rest. Which almost always led to verbal abuse for both of them. Comments regarding their lack of strength or their weak character. The fact that Sky could not possibly be his son for he lacked all of his family's excellent genes and abilities.

An end for me, because there was never anything I could do but watch and later cry myself to sleep. An end for my mother, for she was about to remove herself from the situation permanently. The situation being my father, the marriage, and the abuse.

I have often wondered why. Why stay and allow herself to be treated like an unwanted dog until it was time to fetch the day's paper. Now with some age, maturity, and experiences of my own; I know why, love. Love for me, to be raised in a family with both parents. Love for my brother, hoping he would learn how not to treat those, he said, he loved. Most important, love for my father. For the man she knew he could be. Love that can only be understood by one who has experienced such love. An understanding I pray never to achieve.

Not very long after Sky and I read mother's diary things began to change. Things became even tenser than ever before. Sky and I tried very hard to stay out of the way. Not just father's but mother's as well. But staying out of the way wasn't enough. Our mother's behavior became very strange, for she would do things she knew would anger my father; but she seemed not to care. She became hostile and daring. She began insulting everyone, including Sky and me. But even that was not enough, for the worst was yet to come. For mother got her wish; to some degree anyway.

It started as a regular night in our house. Not long after mother had sent me to bed, I had my usual episode of nightmares. And like always I got up and crept into Sky's room. On my way I heard the screams and other sounds of anger coming from my parent's room knowing the fists were flying and creating the routine black-eyes, swollen lips and other bruises that mother did not try to hide or explain anymore. Partly because everyone knew the source and partly because no one ever came to visit, that didn't know already.

Mother had decided not to be abused anymore and the only way to stop it was to stop daddy. I remember that the sounds were different in this argument. I realized why they were different, mother was arguing back, she was screaming back at father just as loud as he was. This was something we had never heard before. Always in the past, fathers voice and mothers crying was all that could be heard. Or the worst ones were when there were no voices, just the sounds of mother's body being used to rearrange the decor of the room or change the diagram of a room by using her body as a wrecking ball to take out a wall.

No, this particular argument was intended to have a different ending, different because, a new director had written this script. This ending was to be more than just a cliffhanger, it would be the final showing. Mother had been yelling back at father and if he hit her, she would hit him back. She was hurling anything in his direction that got within her reach to prove her point that this show was well and truly over. She was grabbing things off the dresser, off the shelves and finally made her way to the night table where he kept his gun.

Later Sky and I would hear the question asked if mother knew the gun was there all the time or if of the three little drawers to choose from, was just a random selection that made her grab that fatal drawer. We don't know what guided the choice but we know what the end result would be. She found his gun and then it changed from an argument on a large scale to an argument of epic proportions.

She made it known that this was a new day and things were going to be different, from then on there would be no more cowering and bleeding. She would be the woman of her own house and she would be the woman that my father had never met and she would not hesitate to fight back.

Father, underestimating mother's desire to end this phase of her life took two steps toward her; and even through her bloodshot eyes she shot daddy intending to stop him, maybe even kill him who knows. But even on this, her night of retaliation, mother was not to escape unscathed. Mother had just grabbed the gun and started firing. The gun backfired and mother dropped it beside where daddy had fallen on the floor. She was intent on getting away from him, I guess not even realizing what she had done; just wanting to get away before he could hurt her any more.

Call it will power or whatever you will, but daddy had enough strength to pick up the gun and fire it one last time. The bullet entered her back just below her heart, hit her ribcage and bounced around until it reached its final resting-place where it remains till today. In her lower back near her spine.

Mother was so intent on getting away from father that even after she had been shot she managed to get out the door and out of the house. No one knows how she was able to do that and when the extent of her injuries were revealed it was said to be amazing that she was even conscious, let alone able to walk.

Mother left us, she left us in this house, alone with this strange and dangerous man. Yes, a whining, moaning, and bleeding stranger. For at that point, that precise moment, he was no longer my father or anyone that I knew. Just a stranger that lay bleeding and crying on the floor; at the base of a wall smeared with blood. His blood.

My brother stood over him, yelling and screaming at him; telling him that he had gotten what he deserved. Telling him it would serve him right if he died. I stood alone in the corner wondering what to do. I knew I had to get out of the house. Outside in the night air away from the screams, away from the blood on the wall, and away from him. Without ever glancing at Sky and the figure on the floor I followed mothers' trail of blood out the door.

Mother was nowhere in sight. I followed the trail to the edge of our tiny yard where it simply stopped. As if mother had just disappeared. My first and only thought upon arriving at the end of that trail, was where did my mother go and how was I going to get to her, because I could not go looking for her. Play rule number one was never to go past the neighbors' house. So I decided if I could not go past the house then maybe I could go to the neighbor's house to get help.

Strangely enough, I wanted help only to find mother; not the man on our floor bleeding. A man I had no concern for and no thoughts about his life as it was quickly draining out of his body in the form of a never ending red river ruining my mother's beautiful carpet.

I remember I wished for my father, not this stranger on the floor of our house. For my father would not have allowed this to happen. But this awful thing had happened and my father had been the catalyst; or maybe it was Sky and myself.

My mother had told Sky once that she married my father because she was pregnant with him. Then became pregnant with me against my father's wishes; not intentionally of course. But she said father did not allow birth control pills in the house. So it was up to her to find a way to do her wifely duties and not get pregnant all at the same time. We were told these things in an off handed way as if we knew what they meant or we would be able to draw a reasonable conclusion. Actually we had no idea, we simply translated what mother said into meaning it was all our fault. The arguments, the fights or beatings as it were, all of it was laid at our feet.

CHAPTER THREE.....
A NEIGHBORS' FEAR

Our neighbors, Anna and Eric, were awake. Anna was pregnant and having difficulty sleeping. She was on her way back to bed, after some warm milk and conversation with her husband, Eric. Hoping that the warm milk would help her and the baby relax, she decided to make one more attempt at the sometimes evasive pastime known as sleep, when gunshots shattered the stillness of the night. Unsure of the direction or the acuteness of her hearing until I rapped on the door. Thereby, signifying that the impossible had become very possible. That someone in the Stephens household had been shot and maybe dying or already dead.

For like many of our neighbors, they were aware of the abuse but just did not want to get involved. To Anna, it seemed wrong and plain selfish. Many times at night hearing the yelling and screaming coming in through the open windows, she would beg her husband to go knock on the door or at least call the police. His response was always the same, that it was not their business and that they had no right to get involved. But he had also said, when Marie tired of her treatment she would address the problem herself in her own way. Anna would often reply, to herself, that she prayed he was right and that it would happen before her worst fears took shape. Before someone was seriously wounded or killed. On this night, both Anna and Eric would find out how truly accurate they had both been.

The proof that this their worst fear had become a reality, was standing on their doorstep in the form of the Stephens youngest child, Dee who was asking very politely for her mother, and offering her tale of woe as justification for a visit at this ungodly hour.

To my apparent dismay my mother was not there. Not there and they had no idea where she could be, but Anna was not willing to allow me to go traipsing out into the night in my pajamas looking for my mother who she said could be anywhere. So Anna encouraged me to stay with them, at least until they could call someone to come and take charge of the situation and take care of me and Sky. I was not happy with this but was told by Eric that he could not allow me to wander around in the night so Anna held me tucked against her rounded belly as her husband called the police and the ambulance. Feeling very much like a child himself, only being able to tell the dispatcher his assumption of the events that had taken place. Having no idea that quite a few of the horrible things he had tried to erase from his pregnant wife's mind, when her imagination would conjured up all sorts of horrors during many long nights of listening to the garish cries coming thru the window, had actually happened.

The sirens came first, piercing the silent night screaming their anger at a need to be out transporting injured bodies. Eric wanted to wait inside, but Anna insisted on meeting them in front of the Stephens house, not wanting to waste time that an injured and bleeding life may not have. Although I spoke calmly when reciting the events that had taken place in our house, Anna felt that actually things were much worse and that I was obviously in shock.

Police cars and emergency vehicles seemed to appear out of the dense fog.

As the doors flew open and people started emerging from them like a dropped bag spills its contents, all I could do was sit and watch from my comfortable little nest in Anna and Eric's arms where Anna demanded I stay. It seemed very strange that all I could think about was that mother would be angry about all the strangers in the house.

People were roaming all about the house taking pictures and asking questions of Anna and Eric. Questions neither one could answer; but wanted answers to as well.

The answers to these questions lay quietly with us and we were not sure how much to say or not say. We still had no idea where our mother had gone and we did not want her to get in trouble for leaving us alone. Even though our father was at home, his condition was so critical it was asked if he could even be considered aware of us at all.

We were 8 and 11 year old children, who had witnessed sights that no child should ever see, not even as a part of a television show. The police found it difficult to question us but found no other way to obtain the vital information. We became agitated with the police and their many questions because we wanted nothing but our mother.

We were not concerned with the condition of our father. Our only concern was the whereabouts of our mother, not because she left us alone with father; a usual occurrence. But because she left, and did not say when she would return; as she had always done before.

Mother had been located but we would not discover until a week later where she was and how she was when she was found.

Mother was at another neighbor's house, lying on some plastic sheeting in the middle of the floor; like an injured animal rescued from the noon day traffic. She too, like father was taken away in one of those screaming vehicles with bright flashing lights on top.

We were once again left at a neighbor's house while our parents were taken to the hospital and treated for their injuries. Both of which were very serious and could well have been fatal for either or both.

It would be more than two months before we would eavesdrop on a conversation and learn the nature of our mother's injuries. More than a year would pass before we learned of our fathers'. I guess it was thought the less we knew the better off we would be. But there again adults refuse to accept the fact that even though we were not told right away, we kind of figured it out for ourselves.

My mother was considered to be suffering from Post-Traumatic Stress Disorder (PTSD) brought on by long term physical and mental abuse. I guess the shooting incident was considered "self-defense" in legal terms, because mother never had any criminal charges filed against her. Nor did my father although everyone felt that he should have for all the years of abuse to my mother, and Sky for that matter.

Both my parents received extended therapy, both physical and mental. Therapy was also ordered for Sky and myself. Sky always seemed angrier after his session than at other times. I always assumed that was how it was supposed to work. My sessions, from what I remember, were lots of talking and drawing pictures. Sometimes the doctor and I would take turns making up silly stories.

I always tried to tell Mom and Sky about my sessions but neither wanted to listen. Mom, because they were constant reminders of what she had been through. Sky, because he thought they were useless, sense all we did was talk, color pictures and make up stories.

Mother got a divorce, with no question of custody. We did not expect to live with our father and had no desire to.

CHAPTER FOUR.....
MOVING ON....

Our parents were slow to heal physically and psychologically. Mother had a collapsed lung and it took longer than expected for it to heal. She also developed pneumonia and a staph infection in her surgical site and had to stay in the hospital much longer than she wanted too. For weeks our routine was the same, school during the day and evenings spent sitting in the hospital waiting room, eating hospital food that we eventually learn to tolerate.

The nurses avoided us initially, choosing to whisper around corners about the sadness and cruelty of our situation. Sky and I would pretend not to notice them staring and trying to whisper softly and failing. We would just give each other looks across the table, or mostly me trying not to giggle as Sky made silly faces, or mimicked the nurses behind their backs. I now think back and realize this was done to entertain and distract me.

After weeks of this dull routine that wore our grandmother out and bored us to tears, one of the nurses suggested that we volunteer to read to the children in the pediatric units. Nurse Michelle, RN was all her badge said, but to Sky and I she was the best friend a kid could have. She told us she had two little brothers and knew that children bored easily and had to be kept busy. Michelle had no problem with us, it was just that she felt the other nurses were doing more harm than they realized by talking about us that way and she convinced our grandmother to let us try her idea. It would keep us busy and calm the children, especially the ones that did not have family staying with them. Sky refused at first and I went along with him, of course. But away from everyone else, I told Sky that I thought it might be fun and I wanted to try it at least once.

As was his way, Sky gave in for me and I read to the preschool ages and Sky to the older ones. It became our new routine that we would get to the hospital, go see mother for a few minutes because she tired easily and she was still weak from all the blood loss and the infections; then our homework had to be done first and our favorite nurse would check it; then off to read to the children we thought were in worse shape than we were, after all they were in the hospital but we went to Nana Jones house every night.

I began to enjoy the readings as much as the children and realized that I would have loved having someone read to me. Sky met a little girl named Amina that was about my age and he liked her but tried to hide it from everyone even me, but I knew my brother better than he thought I did and I could see the way his face looked when we would talk at night about our day. I also knew that he would not like being teased about it, so I didn't. But I was still a little jealous because I was not interested in sharing my brother with another girl, especially a girl that made his eyes sparkle when talked about her.

Once her lung was on the mend, mother had to deal with the bullet in her back. The doctors explained that the problem was that the bullet in her back could not be removed without risking paralysis. She didn't take the risk.

Strangely enough, the thing she wanted to happen to father, was what almost happened to her.

Mother spent weeks in physical therapy. Regaining her strength took more energy and work than my mother had ever used in her life. At least that's what grandma said, seeing as how mother stayed at home while our father worked.

Our father stayed in the hospital for more than a month. His liver was injured by one of the bullets and he lost a kidney we were later told. He never once asked to see us, or vice versa. I guess those bullets severed more than a lung and a liver.

I really did want to see my father to ask him why this thing happened, but Sky did not want to see him and I could not go see him by myself. My grandmother made it known that she had never liked our father and did not want to see him, so that meant no visits and no chance to ask those questions.

Sometimes when Sky and I were supposed to be reading he would go to the unit and stand outside my mother's room and listen, this was the only way to find out what was going on. No one thought it necessary to tell us anything so we found out in the usual way; eavesdropping. Sometimes I would even ask Nurse Michelle questions when I heard things I did not understand.

I often wonder what made my mother react the way she did and at that time. We never discuss that night or the years before so I guess I will never know.

Our parents had little or no contact after the divorce. Lawyers and the postal system handled everything. A good thing I guess.

My mother's family came and took care of us. We had never spent much time with them or fathers' for that matter. Father always said, "You don't have any business if everyone is in your business". I think that was his way of keeping people from knowing the truth for as long as he possibly could.

Father was an only child and his mother was elderly, she preferred her cats to people. We had gone to visit her once with our parents after she had a bad fall and broke her hip. She did not like children nor my mother and said mean things. Subsequently; she demanded there be no more visits. Our paternal grandmother faded into memory and became like so many other people in our family, just pictures on the walls and tables.

When father was released from the hospital we lost what little contact there was, which consisted of Nana Jones calling the hospital and asking the nurses about his condition, then relaying to us what she felt we needed to know. It would be years later before we heard anything from him. I guess that may have been what was supposed to happen, but I missed him sometimes. I guess I did need him around in some ways, even if I didn't want him in others. I never voiced this to anyone not even to Sky. I knew no one would understand. Sometimes I am not sure I understood it.

Mom had one aunt and a sister in addition to her mother. That was it as far as family. So in the next few months we got to know them and them us.

CHAPTER FIVE.....
ENTERS ASHLEY

We lived with our maternal grandmother, Nana Jones, until mother was well enough to work. A choice mother made out of necessity, not because she wanted to. Especially since she had never worked before. Nana Jones often suggested that mother get a job using what she had learned in college. Mother would always quickly change the subject or she would pretend that she had not heard the suggestion at all. When questioned about her plans, her response would always be I'm thinking or I'm trying to decide. Mother said she had to figure out what she could do and it took her a while and a few different jobs. She tried waiting tables and quit after 3 days because she said the constant walking and standing made her feet hurt, the lifting and carrying plates and trays of food made her wrist hurt and she said the customers were rude. Nana Jones told mother to stop making excuses for being spoiled and lazy because she had never worked before. The truth of the matter that mother never told nana was in the years she was married to my father he had caused her to break her ankle, several of her fingers and her wrist had been broken as well.

Then there was the whole two weeks she worked as a cashier, which she quit because she did not like the way the manager looked at her and was always asking her out on dates. She simply said he was creepy.

Mother was able to get the job because Nana Jones and Aunt Alice like to shop at that store, and knew the manager well. Once, we went to visit her at work to try to offer encouragement as grandmother said. During our visit, we found out why he was so creepy; Mr. Robinson looked kind of like our father so it made sense that he would make mother uncomfortable. Nana Jones told mother she would have to get past her issues with her marriage to our father.

Mother and Nana Jones had a conversation one night when I was supposed to be asleep, but I often had nightmares and would have to get up and move around; side effects of the fights my parents had, that was nana's explanation anyway. Nana told mother that everyone has a past and there was no point in hanging on to it. It was then that I found out that mother sometimes had nightmares about the fights and dreams about the arguments that would keep her up at night. I felt sad inside that mother never talked to us about the things that happened and that I was also having dreams but could not talk about it anymore than my mother could.

Mother's final choice was a position in the bank as a teller. There was little writing involved and mother was sitting on a high stool and she could wear her own clothes.

Once mother started working steadily we moved. It felt a little strange to be in a place we called home and daddy wasn't there. All my life it had been the four of us, now this situation was different for everyone. It took some adjusting for mother who felt stressed and unfocused because she had to learn how to call people to come repair and service things. This had always been daddy's' job.

Mother continued her therapy long after the court appointed time span, she said it was helping her put things in perspective, but to us the therapy seemed to change her greatly. She developed some sort of resentment for Sky and I. She began to act as if we were responsible for everything. We lived near my mother's aunt, who helped her a lot. Aunt Alice, as we called her, loved to cook and was more than happy to have two growing children to cook for.

Mother continued to change however, not for the better, at least that's how we saw it. Mother dated often and always different men. She never seemed interested after a date or two. Mother acted as if she were harboring some hatred for all men. She treated them all harshly and became cruel if they tried to show her any affection. Either because of her treatment or pranks pulled by Sky, they did not hang around long, if at all. Mother acted at times like a crazed vigilante. I felt sorry for those poor souls, being held responsible for things they had not done. I began to feel like a misfit, most of the gentlemen callers that came to the house had not been told about us and was surprised to see us.

After a while we noticed that Aunt Alice did it all; not only was she cooking for us and shopping, but she was paying the bills, caring for the house and for us as well. We had no idea why? Why was mother working but bringing her paycheck home to our aunt? It was a shock to us when we found out that when mother wasn't working; she was drinking heavily. Therefore, we became invisible to her.

Mother acted as if we did not need her, just the financial support she provided. She stated one day that she needed a new focus in her life, something positive to devote her time and energy to. I guess Sky and I were not enough.

She found her new focus point in her younger sister Ashley. When Aunt Ashley arrived to our house she had a little girl, Amber and she was also pregnant. Mother and her sister were close, so close in fact that Ashley had given her daughter mother's middle name Yvonne. Mother began devoting all her time to Ashley and Amber and less time to her drinking; and even less time to Sky and me.

Mother often acted as if she had to take care of Ashley and that she was as responsible for her as she was for us. I overheard a conversation between mother and Nana Jones once that left me very curious; Nana Jones asked mother why she was so intent on taking care of Ashley and why she treated her like royalty. Nana Jones told mother that she was not responsible for Ashley or the things that had happened all those years ago. She told mother that Ashley was not a little girl now and that she understood how things worked and that mother had to stop feeling guilty for Ashley's bad choices. Of course, this made me want to know but would never be brave enough to ask. Sky and I discussed it but could never find out any more about Ashley's "bad decisions".

When the new baby arrived, it was another little girl. Mother acted as if she had given birth to the baby. She would very seldom allow anyone else to do anything for April when she was at home. April was four weeks premature and very small, which provided another reason for mother to ignore Sky and ignore me. I loved them all and I think they loved me. But the love I desperately wanted to gain was farther away than China. I tried to get close to Aunt Ashley but she never seemed to return my feelings. At least not in a way that I could understand at the time.

Then began my boundless love for my brother and his for me. It seemed to be; us against the world. My brother became my replacement for everyone that I felt I had lost one way or another. I needed someone to love and someone to love me, just for me. Selfish? Maybe, but at the time I didn't think so and somehow my feelings remain unchanged. We felt we only had each other and maybe we did.

Our birthdays, Christmas, Easter and all the other special days came and went, without much acknowledgement from our mother. After a while we stopped being concerned. Those days just blended into all the others. Mother had a focus, things and people that were important to her and it definitely did not include my brother or myself.

Sky and I learned how to make our own fun, how to entertain ourselves and each other and stay out of mother's way. We continued this way until our mundane existence was reduced to emotional carnage in the form of Charles Caravelle.

CHAPTER SIX...
CLOUDS OF CHANGE

Charles Caravelle, the next phase of torment, will forever be remembered as the ultimate evil. I remember being told he was a friend of the family. For a while he was around all the time. He was always at our house. He seemed to spend as much time at our house as we did.

I knew Sky's curiosity would get the better of him sooner or later and he would ask how mother and Charles knew each other. Because Charles loved to talk and would talk to anyone, he had no problems answering Sky's many questions.

We acquired intelligence through Sky's slick interrogation skills. Come to find out, mother and Charles knew each other from mother's brief stint in college. Turns out, our mother was an artist and had been extremely talented. She was also very gifted with decorating and therefore had received an Art scholarship. Sometime during their second or third year in college mother met our father during his senior year. As mother and father became closer she began to care less about college, less about her degree and less about her desires to paint and decorate.

It was our fathers' desire to one day own his own business and he wanted to be in charge of every aspect of his business, so he was after a Business degree. According to Charles, father had taken extra classes on investing, accounting and finance so that he could manage all his own affairs or oversee them.

Charles told us that Art had been mother's greatest passion until a new one arrived. This passion came in the form of a tall dark possessive and brooding stranger that sat in the back of mother's Economics class.

Charles told us that he remembered meeting our mother in the college bookstore.

Mother came in while Charles was telling us about their time in college and surprisingly she joined in with the story telling.

Mother told us that she liked his smile and his carefree attitude. She told us she was not attracted to him, just fascinated by him. She enjoyed his conversation and he made her laugh. Especially when he would make up silly stories, like the one about the revenge of the dust bunnies on his mom when she dusted the house, we all laughed for a while about that one.

Charles said that he and mother took a few classes together and became good friends and that he loved making mother laugh. Charles said that the one class mother did not like was the class that father was in, which is probably why she was drawn to him as more of a distraction but it turned into something more than she planned. He said mother never knew that she would become a fly caught in father's web and that he was one of the most dangerous types of spiders.

We found out that Charles' nickname for mother was curious George because she was forever asking questions and "investigating" things.

It seemed Charles was a permanent fixture in our living room. He made mother laugh and smile, something Sky and I had not seen in many months. He also entertained us and brought fun and smiles to our house. For this we were okay with him being around so much.

During his visits Charles always made it a point to speak to Ashley, but there never seemed to be any conversation between them. Sky said it was because Ashley liked Charles in the adult way that women liked men. I felt their lack of conversation was due to the fact that Ashley really did not like him, because Charles paid more attention to us than her. We would soon find out, that we were both wrong, of course.

Charles never seemed to mind us being around like his parade of predecessors. This added to his favor with us. He often told mother that we (Sky and I) should get out more. Do more things that children our age did, instead of spending so much time at home. But there was a reason we were not allowed to venture far from home. We had duties to perform, duties that went along with maintaining the little fantasy world that my mother had created for Ashley and for herself.

Sky was the butler and I was the built-in nanny, we both waited to be told that we were going to be wearing black and white uniforms. It became a kind of joke between us, trying to figure out what a male Cinderella would be called.

We never really went anywhere because we were always doing our chores, which was whatever Aunt Ashley needed done for the girls or for herself. I guess because of his continued comments and encouragement mother began to relent.

Occasionally, for entertainment mother would allow Charles to spend time alone with Sky and I. Sky and Charles seemed to bond instantly. I spent most of my time with the girls, they almost seemed to be my girls. Every afternoon and every weekend I was with them, and Sky was with Charles.

One afternoon Sky came home after being out with Charles all afternoon and came to my room, he said we needed to go outside and play. This was exciting because for us, "going out to play", was our code to each other that we needed to talk away from everyone. So we went out in the yard and Sky told me he knew what "bad decisions" Nana Jones was talking about.

When mother was in college Ashley would sometimes be allowed to go visit her on long weekends or when their parents wanted to go away for the weekend. Ashley and mother were very close and Ashley loved being around all the college kids.

While visiting mother Ashley decided that she was in love with Charles and wanted to be his girlfriend, although she was four years younger than him. So Ashley decided to let Charles know how she felt and began dressing differently and talking differently around him. She even went so far as to sneak into his room one night to wait for him. Ashley borrowed some of mother's lingerie and climbed into Charles bed to wait for him and give him a surprise, instead, when Charles came back to his room he told Ashley that she was just a little girl and to go home and take off her sister's underwear. Ashley was insistent that she was in love with him and that she was the best woman for him. Charles said some things that hurt her feelings and her pride then took her back to mother's place. I never found out what was said because, mother came to the door and told us to come in and get started on our chores. Somehow we never managed to finish that particular conversation and I felt like that piece of information was very important but could not say why.

One afternoon Charles asked mother if he could take us out to his ranch in the country. He had a huge place with lots of horses and other animals. A zoo of sorts, one might say. It was a light snow that day, and I guess if I believed there was such a thing as omens, then that would have been considered a bad one. I did not like where he lived, it was too far out. Too far away from everything that felt right to me. But as Sky had said earlier, we were getting away from the house for a change and away from the norm.

That day we met Charles's housekeeper, Olivia. She liked to be called Libby. Libby was a heavyset black woman with big soft brown eyes that seemed to sparkle when she smiled. I loved her instantly. She seemed to sense my loneliness, and became my friend. Libby was a very spiritual person and she prayed a lot. She would always say that she believed in the power of prayer. Libby was different from anyone Sky and I had ever met. She had a strong faith and a deep love for God. Things alien and totally unfamiliar to us. We were not raised in a home where God was discussed or mentioned on a regular basis. Sky was not comfortable with Ms. Olivia's constant references to God and the bible. She talked about God all the time and most of her sentences would start with, "The Word says…" It did not take long for us to learn that by the "the word" she meant the bible.

She had a way of putting people at ease that I had never seen before. She was very smart, she could always tell when Sky and I were funning with her or just not telling the truth at all. She could take control of a situation and make you feel completely cared for. She controlled every aspect of Charles' household and most of the time I thought she controlled Charles as well.

That first weekend and every one after that she gave me what I wanted and needed most, someone to care and make me feel that I mattered. She would put the girls down for a nap, I would sit with my head in her lap and she would tell me stories about her childhood. How her mother had cared for a wealthy family for most of her life, and that she and her mother found their work fulfilling and that they were "good at it ".

Ms. Olivia would either read to me or tell me stories about people in the bible and all the things that they did because God told them too. This would make Sky uncomfortable and he would always find a reason or an excuse to leave the room. Time always seem to fly as I would lay in her lap or at her feet listening to her stories. Listening to the life and times of this woman who knew so much more about life, love and God than Sky thought was right for anyone to know.

Once after a visit I asked Sky why he never liked Libby's stories or when she would read from the bible to us? He said that if God was real and had the kind of power that Libby spoke about, He would not have let those bad things happen to our mother and He would have stopped our father before he hurt mother all those nights long ago. Sky said he felt like God should not punish the good people, only the bad ones and because we had all suffered a type of punishment for things that we had never done, he had a problem with Libby's God. Sky's words confused me more than Ms. Olivia's did when it came to God and "the Word" as she called it.

I would dread seeing Charles come into the kitchen, because I knew he was ready to go. But I never was. Olivia would always make Charles promise to be careful driving and to bring me to visit again. A promise I would eventually regret his keeping. Charles seemed more delighted about my fondness of Ms. Olivia than I felt comfortable with, for reasons that would not avail themselves to me at that time.

Often on the way home, I couldn't stop talking long enough for Sky to get a word in edgewise. But he was very happy that I had found a friend and would simply sit and listen to a play by play of my weekend, most of which he already knew because he was there but he would listen anyway. He also soon realized he would acquire a better chance to tell me about his day with Charles if he waited until later when some of my excitement wore off.

We made many more trips to Ms. Olivia's house. I say this because it felt more like her house than his. It was always Sky, the girls (Amber & April), and myself. Every weekend to Charles' house to see Ms. Olivia. Libby, her childhood pet name, always found a way to keep the girls occupied. Something I could never do. Maybe that was another one of those things that you learn with age that Libby was always telling me about.

I would spend my time either walking around behind Libby step for step or sitting in a chair eating something that she had made that tasted too good to just be called food.

I remember once during a visit I started thinking about the things Sky had told me and I was curious so I asked Libby how she dealt with disappointment or having bad things happen to her. Her response again confused me more than I already had been. Libby said that she prayed and talked to God about everything. She said that when she was young her mother did the same thing and she often wondered if God got tired of her mother always calling His name.

But Libby explained to me that God wanted us to call on Him and come to him in prayer instead going to other people. When I asked why, she told me because other people could only guess, but God always knows. Libby said, sometimes things people tell you may be based on how they feel and not on the truth or the facts. Libby would always say, "There is power in prayer." This one I never got and could make no sense of. But she kept talking and I had to pay attention to keep up with the conversation. But I knew I would be lying in bed later thinking about all these things Libby had told me. Libby said that God had a way of using our experiences to make us better prepared for what was coming and strong enough to deal with what life gave us. She said one of her favorite scriptures was Philippians 4:13 "I can do all things through Christ who strengthens me."

Although I did not understand a great deal of what Libby was telling me, something inside me made me feel like I could trust everything she told me and believe it to be true. Once Libby knew that I could read, she gave me a little bible of my own. I loved it because it was small enough to put in my little backpack, it was purple my favorite color and it was something that was all mine. She gave one to Sky as well, but he managed to leave it at the ranch every time we left to go home.

Charles would pay Sky to do odd jobs. His way of giving Sky money without mother complaining that he was spoiling him and kept Sky out of Libby's kitchen so he did not have to always listen to her stories. This also provided Charles with the opportunity to spend more time alone with me, which he began doing, often. I did not like the idea at first. But I soon began to think that maybe I was judging him unfairly. After all he had been taking us to his house, giving my brother money, and making it possible for us to have more fun than we had had in a long time. The more time I spent around Charles the more I began to trust him, my second mistake of many as I would very soon discover.

Libby and I would talk and I would often ask her to repeat stories that she had already told me before, but she never complained she would simply do as I asked. My favorite became the story of Esther and the king. I loved how she continued to love her uncle even after she became queen and that she stayed the special person she had always been. Libby would say that Esther was humble. Another one of those things that would keep me up late thinking.

Libby said she knew I was learning as I listened and that my understanding of God would grow just as my love for God would. Sky became as fond of Libby as I was even though he did not enjoy her stories and reading as much as I did, but he was ever mindful to show her much respect and would sometimes even ask an occasional question which proved he was listening a little.

CHAPTER SEVEN.....
CHARLES' TRUE COLORS

As I began to spend more and more time around Charles, I noticed a change in the way he acted toward me. Sometimes I would catch him staring at me, when I asked why he would say something about how pretty I was. He would say things to me sometimes that I felt uncomfortable with, but I would give him a strange look and he would change the subject. Sometimes without warning he would touch my hair or let it slip through his fingers. One of the oddest thing he would do would be to stand next to me and inhale deeply as if he were trying to memorize my scent. There never seemed to be a reason to tell Libby or Sky since I didn't want to be a tattletale or a big baby. Besides there really wasn't anything to tell, or was there.

The weekend in question was like so many others. The usual trip to the ranch to see Libby, but somehow this weekend I was the only one going. I was glad because it meant I would have more time alone with Libby. When I questioned Charles about my being alone, he told me some far-fetched tale about Ashley and mom taking the girls shopping so I could have a free weekend. He said that Sky was working. I knew something was wrong because Ashley was always saying how much easier it was to shop without the girls tagging along.

But I trusted Charles to tell me the truth. Another mistake. On this particular weekend Ashley had taken the girls to see their father. But Charles knew I was not aware of this, so he used my ignorance to his advantage.

We took a different route to the ranch this weekend or maybe I was so busy contemplating my time with Libby, which I never paid attention to the route we took. Charles told me he wanted to show me his secret place from his childhood. Everything in the very fiber of my being told me I should be afraid, but I felt I had no reason to fear this man or distrust him.

We came upon a lake surrounded by trees. There was a small group of trees in the center, all close together like they were in a huddle. One of the trees had a big box in the very top. Charles told me it was his childhood tree house. From the road the treehouse could not be seen, nor the short little narrow road that lead up to it. As we approached what was really a wide dirt trail my palms began to sweat, I shrugged it off thinking it was the summer heat.

He parked the van and got out. I sat there staring out the window, listening to the little voice inside my head telling me we should not be here. He came around and opened the door for me to get out. For a moment I just sat there staring at him. He said we were only going to stay a few minutes then I would be going to see Libby. I climbed out and found it difficult to stand, my legs were shaky and weak from nervousness.

He began to walk away while he was telling me about his fishing trips to this spot and I had to follow him just hear what he was telling me. He pointed to an area several feet away that looked like the water disappeared, he said there was a part of the lake where the water ran over a tumble of rocks and made a little waterfall. He said we could see it later and even swim if I wanted to. We approached the tree that held the tree house.

As we climbed the ladder, narrow boards nailed into the tree trunk, I began to sweat more profusely. This tree house had everything; a bed, a desk and chair; even real panes in the windows and a mirror on the wall. The only thing missing was the air conditioning.

I sat at the desk and Charles on the bed. He started to unbutton his shirt, mumbling something about the heat. I was involved in a paperback I had found in one of the desk drawers.

He walked up behind me and began massaging my shoulders and neck. He started talking but I was not listening at first, then when I finally realized that he was speaking to me; he was saying something about how pretty I was, and that very soon boys would start to notice me. He said that most of the boys nowadays already knew things that I didn't. He said that he didn't want me to feel left out, so he was going to teach me the things that boys liked for girls to know. I told him I didn't need to know any of those things because I didn't like boys at all, except my brother, so it didn't matter much to me. Besides I was only eleven years old.

He told me that if he started teaching me now, by the time I started liking boys I would know how to do everything they wanted. He told me that these "classes" would be our little secret and that I shouldn't tell anyone because they would not understand. Charles said that he was glad that he had waited for me and had not chosen Ashley. He said that was why she was so jealous of me, because she knew he liked me more than her. That by the time he met mother and Ashley, she was too old for him to teach her what she needed to know. Something about his comments made me think that something was very very wrong with us being here alone and I needed to be anywhere but there with him.

I started to get nervous again and told him I was ready to go. That I wanted to see Libby, that she would be worried and wondering where we were. The look in his eyes told me that was the least of his concerns at that time.

He said that after we spent some time at the treehouse, we could go for a swim and cool off in the waterfall, at that point I was no longer interested in swimming or the waterfall especially if I had to be alone with Charles and have him looking at me that way.

Charles began walking toward me. Somehow during the conversation we had switched places. I forgot which end of the tree house I was on and began backing away from him. When I bumped into the bed I was off balance and I fell backward, Charles took advantage of my clumsiness. He hopped on me like a house cat on a mouse. He kept telling me these were things that I needed to know.

He said he was saving my mother the uncomfortable task of teaching me. All the while he was tearing off my clothes. He ripped off my shirt the same as my bra. Saying I didn't need that ridiculous article of clothing anyway. He said something about women being naked and free like the bible days. I was disgusted that he would use the bible to try to justify his need to make a point, especially this point. I was wearing a skirt, at his request. He snatched at it and it tore like paper in his grasp.

I was kicking and screaming, he smiled and told me I was wasting my time because no one would hear me. He took great pride in telling me that the lake was surrounded by ten acres of land and that he owned it all, therefore, there was no chance of anyone hearing me. I think he was laughing at my futile attempts to fight him off. I continued to fight, even though he had this wild animal like glare in his eyes; and I knew I could not get away until he decided to let me go. Which would not be soon enough to suit me. But I still felt that I could not just lay there and I didn't. He was sweating profusely, the combination of the heat and my constant struggling made it unavoidable. He penetrated my little body with such force that I felt all the air leaving my lungs as if it were being sucked out by a high powered machine. I felt as if I would faint from the pain alone. It was very hard to breathe. Shock I presume. I never knew one could experience such pain. I was lightheaded and everything was blurry, including his face hovering above mine. But there was no doubt in my mind that he was there.

He kept talking, more so to himself than to me. He talked as if to give himself encouragement that what he was doing was right and for the right reasons. When it was over he just lay there staring at the ceiling. I saw my chance and took it. I jumped up grabbed the first thing I saw, his shirt, and ran almost falling down the ladder.

I could hear him laughing and saying there was nowhere to go; and if I did who would believe the lies I would tell.

I was crying and running. Running and crying. I was running with this new found energy. I am not sure where I was running to, but I knew in my heart that if I could get to Libby she would make everything alright.

I tried to remember which direction the waterfall was in because I could not remember which direction we had come from, but I knew the waterfall was in the other direction. I could not remember anything but the look on Charles' face and the sound of his laughter and I just wanted to get away from here and get to Libby.

CHAPTER EIGHT.....
SAFE WITH LIBBY

I kept running until my sides and my stomach hurt, and I thought I would throw up. I was so tired, but I knew I could not stop; not just yet. I thought about just lying down in the grass and praying to God to let me die. Then I saw it, the most beautiful sight in the world. Libby's jeep parked in the middle of the field. I stopped and looked both ways as if I was expecting a gigantic truck to come from nowhere. Instead I saw Libby bent over in the grass picking berries. I felt that God had put Libby out there because He knew I needed her. And I thanked Him for it the way she had taught me too.

I started yelling her name and screaming so she would turn around. But as I feared Libby had her headphones on. I then regretted that gift to her from Sky and myself.

She told me that she wore them when she was alone to take the edge off the aloneness she felt at times. I ran toward her screaming even though I knew she could not hear me. I screamed until I was almost hoarse, but no matter how loud or how much I screamed she could not hear me. But I knew if I could just get close enough to get her attention, I would be okay, I would be safe. The way I was always safe with Libby. As I continued to drag my tired and hurting body across that field, all I could think about was, why me? What had I done that was so wrong that I deserved this awful thing to happen to me? What was going to happen to me when my mother and Sky found out, would I be in trouble would I not be allowed to visit Libby anymore? I began to wonder if Sky would be mad at me because I let this happen. I was trying to figure out how to explain this to him so he would not be angry with me, and the more I tried the worse I began to feel. All these questions ran through my mind as I ran through the field, running to the one person that I thought would be able to fix this mess I had made.

Then she started toward her jeep, a gift from Charles. I did not want her to leave me out there with him. For although I could not see him, I knew he was out there somewhere because I could smell him. A product of my imagination fueled by fear, maybe but I did not want to stay out here and find out. I wanted to leave this place and never come back, I wanted Libby to see me, to hear me and help me as she always had.

I kept screaming and running toward her and waving my arms hoping to get her attention. Libby got in her jeep and started to pull away, then suddenly she stopped. She got out and turned in my direction. As I got closer Libby began to run toward me. Imagine that. Libby, all 230 pounds of her, running. Had it not been for my fear and pain, I would have laughed myself silly. When Libby finally reached me I was so breathless I could not speak, but something in her eyes told me that I didn't have to. I could tell she suspected what had happened and maybe even who was responsible. But I saw something else, something I had never seen visit her face before. I had no idea what it was and thought maybe I imagined it, but it was something new for both of us.

I grabbed a hold of Libby and swore that I would never let her go and by the way she was holding on to me, she was probably feeling the same. We stood there wrapped around each other. Then it dawned on me, that she was praying and crying too. Could she be afraid that someone would blame her for this, that maybe it was her fault? No, it was all my fault, someway somehow I had caused this and I was going to be in trouble with everyone and Sky was going to be so angry with me. All these thoughts tumbled through my aching head as we headed back to her jeep. What was going to happen to me, what would my mother and Ashley say. They all loved Charles and would never believe that he would do anything wrong, no this was going to be all my fault.

We got back to her jeep and drove away. She said absolutely nothing all the way back to the house. When we reached the house she helped me from the jeep and up the steps to the kitchen door. I guess with my feeling of security also came exhaustion, because I could barely put one foot in front of the other. I hesitated at the back door to the kitchen, I did not want to see Sky looking like this but more than that I did not want to see Charles ever again.

We entered the kitchen and I began instantly looking around for Charles, he was nowhere in sight. I guess he was afraid to show his face now that I was with Libby. I turned around to face Libby and there was a look of horror on her face I had never seen before. I looked down and saw the trail of blood I had left on her freshly mopped and waxed kitchen floor.

I immediately began to apologize. I promised faithfully to clean it up if she let me rest a minute. I started to cry again, how is it that I keep managing to mess up everything. It seemed that I could do nothing right and yet I had always tried to do just that, but these recent events proved that I was not as good a person as Libby had told me I was and that the good heart she said I had was actually bad and the truth coming out in every possible way. The last thing I wanted was to be scolded, especially by Libby. The look on Libby's face made me want to cry harder but there were no more tears. She gathered me up in her arms and whispered soft soothing words in my ear. Just what I needed, my Libby. I started trying to tell her what had happened and that I was not being bad on purpose that things just kept happening and I could not stop them. I was trying hard to apologize to Libby about the stuff with Charles and the mess on the floor and when I blubbered something about the tree house and Charles and how he had hurt me, Libby sat me down and put her hands over her ears and begged me to spare her the vivid details of what she already knew. She began to say a poem that I had heard her speak before. I knew it was something from the bible, but I was never sure what.

Something about her words and her face was louder than my heartbeat and I had to sit there and just listen to it replay in my head for a moment. She already knew, but how, she was not at the tree house and I had to run to get to her in the field so how did she 'already know'.

I felt like I had missed something somewhere and no matter how I tried I could not figure out where I lost track and what I lost but I knew I was missing a big piece of something and this time it was not Libby's cake that I was missing a piece of.

As I sat there staring at Libby and having her watch me, I realized that Libby was aware, that the piece I was missing was right there in front of me. Could it be that Libby knew I was a bad person and had just tried to ignore it or that she was waiting for me to show it all along. I began to wonder if she knew, did Sky know too. I felt like I had lost everything and there was nothing I could do about it.

CHAPTER NINE.....
A MOTHER'S LOVE

As much as Libby did not want to believe that Charles could do such a thing, all the proof she would ever need was sitting in the chair in front of her; bleeding on her kitchen floor.

She cleaned me up using all the tenderness and love she could muster. Telling me that I was going to be fine. That God and she would protect me from further harm, which she was going to call my mother and have her come take me to get some proper medical treatment.

Libby kept talking but I was still thinking that she was thinking this was my doing and that I did this to get Charles in trouble and I had to tell her that I was not doing these things on purpose. But I would not get an opportunity to explain because as I opened my mouth to speak the back door opened and anything I would have said left me as a shadow fell across the floor that I knew could only belong to one person, the person I never wanted to see.

Charles came into the kitchen and was coming toward me when I started to scream, Libby turned toward him and yelled at him "Stop right there mister", he ignored Libby and started yelling at me. Asking where I had been that he had been driving around in the heat looking for me. Libby shouted at him so loud the windows rattled and the walls shook. He took a step in my direction and Libby stepped between us and pulled out a gun.

He stopped in his tracks and stared at Libby like a frightened deer caught in headlights. She told him that she knew what had happened and that she was not going to let him near me.

Charles looked at Libby then at me and started to shake his head and tell Libby that she had it all wrong, that he had done nothing and that I was making up stories like all children do. Libby told him to hush his lying. She told him that she knew the truth before I ever opened my mouth. She told Charles that I did not need to tell her anything she could see with her own eyes, old though they were they could see the truth, especially when it was written in blood.

I am not sure if it was her voice or her face that made him be quiet, but I know the gun made him back away from both of us. He took a few wobbly steps backward then dropped in the nearest chair and continued to stare at Libby as she picked up the phone. She kept her body in between him and me. She called the police and my mother, while he kept begging her to wait to let him explain.

Libby was having none of it, she shut him down like she had pulled his plug from the socket. While he sat there just barely breathing and staring at the floor, Libby took me to another room. She took me back to the bathroom and started to wash me again. She was mumbling to herself and washing me like I was a gravy spot on her linen tablecloth. I sat quietly through the scrubbing knowing somehow nothing I said would make a difference, she knew how dirty I was and she was going to get me clean one way or another. I sat there being washed and rinsed, scrubbed and rubbed till it burned my skin and I was pretty sure I would have no skin by the time she felt I was clean. But I sat quietly knowing this is what happens to all dirty little girls.

When my mother arrived she had Aunt Ashley in tow as always. Libby introduced herself and invited them in. Libby gave Ashley an accusing stare, and I am almost positive that Ashley knew why and what the look was for, because Ashley did not say a word. She just kind of slithered into the house, and took the seat that was offered without so much as a second glance at Libby or anyone else.

Libby started to tell mother what had happened in the nicest way she could think of trying very hard not to use the word rape. But this particular day mother was slow to catch any hints, and began asking Libby a lot of questions that it was clear Libby did not want to answer.

Before it got too embarrassing; Ashley got enough nerve to speak and asked where Charles was, and why wasn't I ready to leave. Libby continued with her explanations as if she did not hear either one of them speaking to her. She was intent to tell them her story and they were going to listen, interested or not; willing or not.

I was about to enter the room and attempt an explanation myself when the doorbell rang. Giving me the escape I needed because I had no idea what, if anything, I was going to say.

Or would be able to say with my mother and Ashley staring at me, as I am sure they would have been. Libby got up and left the room. Mother and Ashley sat there whispering. Libby reentered with two men in uniform. There was also a third one that wore a suit, he stood away from the other two watching everyone.

Mother interrupted wanting to know why the police were there. Libby tried very hard to explain. But mother would only listen long enough to hear the words rape, Charles, and Dee then she started telling Libby to shut up. She was saying that she did not believe anything that she had heard. That Libby was just a senile old woman with an overactive imagination. That this was some story I had conjured up because I really didn't like Charles anyway. But the police took control at this point and changed everything. What I did not know was that he saw what she did not, that Libby was not just telling my story she was also telling her own.

Libby was so calm it was almost scary, she just keep talking even though it seemed no one was really listening. She was talking and her voice was starting to get louder and she was wringing her hands and looking at the floor like something awful was happening right there on the floor in front of her. I wanted to go to her and hug her like she would always do me when my voice let her know that I was sad. But I was still too afraid to show myself.

While the police were trying to calm Libby, mother found Charles sitting in the kitchen and told him she did not believe anything Libby had said. She told him that I had made up this wild tale and found some way to manipulate Libby into believing me, and that Libby only thought she believed it. Mother told Charles that she was going to find me and make me tell the truth. Charles told her that he wanted to tell her, his side of the story; but mother was so busy talking she wasn't listening.

I was in the hallway outside Libby's room, just off the living room and I could hear them talking without having to stand there under Ashley's' vicious stare. I knew no matter what anyone said Ashley would blame me. She would sit there and give me one of her accusing stares as if every word that came out of my mouth was a lie. Strangely enough I was never the one to make up things or tell tales, my life had been bad enough I did not see a need to make it worse by creating stories.

CHAPTER TEN.....
LIBBY'S TALE OF WOE

Libby had removed her apron in the dining hall to receive her guests, which was her custom. Sky entered the room by way of the hall from the other door, so he had no way of knowing I was there listening. He decided to back up, stay in the hall and listen. For he knew as soon as they started talking, if it were dealing with some adult issue mother would make him leave the room.

By the time mother returned with Charles behind her, the police had everyone calmed down. They began asking questions. Realizing very quickly that mother and Ashley arrived after the "incident" as they called it, and only knew what they had been told by Libby, the questions began with Libby.

Libby began to tell the police the same story she had tried to tell mother, with some added details.

She started by apologizing to mother for allowing this awful thing to happen. She went on to say that she felt something was wrong but she wasn't sure. She stated that she should have known something like this was bound to happen because she had seen all the signs. When asked by one of the officers what exactly she meant, she started by saying that Charles was not a bad person he was just confused and needed someone to guide him on the right road. She then started to tell them about some of the things he would say about little children when he was out helping her with the shopping or other chores. She said she had noticed that he had an unusual fondness for little girls and tried to make herself think it was because he was single and childless, but in her heart she knew better.

She said her heart told her and her memories as well, no one was sure what that meant but when she looked at the expression on Ashley and mother's face it helped her get back on track with her explanation.

Libby said she thought if she could keep him away from things that might get him into trouble he would be okay. It was at this time he was offered the sale of the Ranch. He said he wanted to buy it because one of his buddies needed to get rid of it. So she encouraged Charles to buy it. It would keep him out of the city and away from temptations that might bring out the part of him she wished to stay hidden. After a few months at the ranch he began to calm down and she felt that it had been her imagination that made her think those things before and that Charles was okay. She put those thoughts away and planned to never let them resurface again. Besides several of their associates had children that had been to the ranch and had spent considerable time there and nothing had happened and she had detected no change in Charles or his behavior.

Libby told them that when Charles ran into his old college buddy Maria Stephens he was very nonchalant about her children. He mostly talked about their college days and the fun they had when they were young. He said that he felt that Maria and her children could use a friend especially her son, he never really mentioned the daughter except to say that Maria had one. He asked if Libby would mind the children in the house occasionally on the weekends to get them away from their house for a while. Libby stated she would be fine with that, especially since it had been almost a year since she had had any children around. Charles told her he wanted to do it for the children to keep them from being babysitters and butlers all the time. She then began encouraging him to bring them and to ask if they could spend the day.

She said that Charles had started behaving differently after the third or fourth visit of the children to the ranch. She spoke as if she was telling one of her stories and not talking directly to someone. Her voice had that faraway quality to it that I knew so well.

She first noticed the change when he began talking in his sleep.

Libby said she has always had trouble sleeping, so often at night she would walk around the house, or clean and dust when she could not rest. She told them that on several different occasions she had been startled by strange voices in the house at night. When she went to investigate, she found that the voices were coming from Charles' study where he often fell asleep. She knocked, but got no answer.

Upon entering the room, she found Charles talking in his sleep and doing things that she had only heard young men did, but had never seen. She said she never thought Charles could be that type of young man. He was also calling Dee's name in his sleep while he did these things that she was sure were unhealthy and would cause blindness (so she was told).

The next morning at breakfast following the first incident, she tried to ask questions but Charles became defensive. After that she never said anything about what she began hearing on a regular basis. But she did tell Charles to mind his daily activities, because they were causing him to talk in his sleep. She would often catch him staring at the child when they came to visit, he would always act as if nothing had happened when he would realize she was watching him. She sat him down once and told him that if he was having thoughts about Dee that she was too young and that it would only cause trouble. He would laugh and say that she was letting her imagination get the best of her.

It was at this time that old ghosts started to haunt her. She tried to blame it on being old-fashioned and not knowing how things worked in the world today. But that would not settle her restless thoughts. She knew something was wrong and may get worse but she did not want to harass Charles with her feelings of dismay, especially if they were groundless. Libby said the look on Charles's face was the mirror image of one that she had faced as a young woman and she knew the problems it would cause if left unmanaged. Charles would say 'you worry too much' or 'there is nothing to worry about'. But in her heart she knew trouble was coming and Charles was right in the middle. She also knew there would be very little she would be able to do to stop it, or him.

That morning he called to say that Dee would be coming out to the ranch alone, that he and Dee would be leaving the city later than usual. But when she tried to call back to inquire about delaying supper, Maria told her that Charles and Dee had left for the ranch already. She tried not to make too much of it but her mind would not let it rest. She wanted to believe that it was her imagination getting active in her old age, but Libby had always relied on her gut instinct to guide her and this time should have been no different. If she had listened to her heart and not her head, this would not have happened.

She tried to go about her business as usual, trying to ignore the constant tugging in her mind that something awful was happening somewhere, and it would change all their lives forever.

To hopefully keep her mind occupied, she decided to make fruit pies for dinner. That would mean she would have to pick fresh berries. The policemen had sat quietly listening to the story Libby told realizing she was trying to assuage some of her own guilt if she could just find out where she went wrong. The one officer that stood alone in the corner watching everyone, watching Libby as she spun her tale, was clearly in charge. He had eyes of steel gray. The kind of eyes that you never forget once you've seen them or been held in their gaze.

Even though I was in another room listening, I could feel the iron grip of control he had over the room and everyone in it including my mother, whom no one could control.

Libby went on telling her story while we all listened, caught up in the web of the tale she weaved. She said she put on her old apron with the big pockets. It was also the one that had a special pocket for the handgun she always carried when she was out picking berries, and away from the safety of the house.

I could feel the shift in the room as everyone realized she was getting to the part of the story that they all wanted to hear. Even now in my mind I can hear the smooth slide of my mother's jeans on the velvet covering of the couch as she eased forward to the edge of her seat.

Libby said she had been in the berry patch about an hour when the heat became unbearable and she decided it was best that she leave before she had a heat stroke or something thereof Mr. Charles was always raving about. Especially when she spent too much time in the sun. She was getting into her jeep, preparing to drive away; when something moving in the rearview mirror caught her attention.

She was thinking it was another one of those nasty poacher people she had had to deal with, the reason for her pistol. But after some focused attention she realized that it wasn't a poacher at all, but a girl in a long dress that did not fit her very well. Then the real truth hit her like a slap in the face.

It was a child, her precious Dee; out in this blistering heat in that ugly frock and barefooted, something Dee's mother never allowed. But the more she watched the more she realized that something was wrong with her. Libby got out of the jeep and stood to look at the child without the glare of the mirror and she felt it before she saw it. The tugging at the corners of her mind, that had plagued her the better half of the day was here and just as she feared all their lives were about to be altered, actually had already been altered.

At this point Libby started to run toward Dee because she felt she needed to get to her right away. As she got closer to her, Libby knew in her heart what had happened but she tried to make logic overrule her heart.

By this time Sky could listen no more, he ran into the room and demanded to see his sister. For he knew if he could talk to Dee or at least just see her he would know if this whole sordid mess was an old woman's overactive imagination, or some terrible nightmare come to life. Because he had to know the truth. One should know all the facts before drawing a conclusion or passing judgment.

Mother became infuriated at the mention of the word rape, but just as she was about to speak; some of the words that Charles had spoken earlier came back to her. She suddenly became very quiet and began to stare at Charles. Began to notice his posture, his downcast eyes; as though he was awaiting the appearance of some great happening there in the plush carpet.

And when by chance he did glance up, gone was the wild sparkle in his eyes that had always made her attracted to him. Instead it was replaced by a pained expression that spoke, yelled utter and complete guilt. Mother glanced at Ashley and found she was also watching Charles. Mother wished she could read Ashley's mind if only for a moment, because the look on Ashley's face was one she had never seen before and it frightened her. At that moment Ashley looked at Maria and they both knew that everything they had heard that day was true.

Finally, I gathered the nerve to enter the room and meet all these questioning eyes that had been diligently awaiting my arrival. I met mother's eyes first, then Ashley's. They were both watching me just as they had watched Charles before I entered the room. Looking for some sign. A glint of untruth, a speck of doubt for them to hold to. Even though mother had received a confession from Charles himself, if she would only allow her mind to take hold. She still needed some other form of proof or disproof. Something she was hoping to acquire from me or my presence.

CHAPTER ELEVEN.....
A BROTHER' REVENGE

Mother asked me to tell them what events had taken place that day, she wanted me to give her firsthand details of what Charles and I had done after we left the house. Thereby implying that I had been a willing partner is his little adventure. But before I could speak, before I could even draw my breath to speak, the detective, the policeman with the steel gray eyes intervened. He had Charles escorted to another room by one of the other officers, I guess everyone but my mother and Ashley were uncomfortable with him in the same room.

Mother was still trying in her own way to get me to say something other than what I had planned to say. The detective quieted mother with merely a glance of those piercing gray eyes. He had asked very few questions before my aunt interrupted to say that I needed medical attention immediately. My mother was about to speak when Ashley placed her hand on mother's arm and told her that I needed to be checked for any permanent damage or possible diseases. What she really wanted to say was that if Charles had really raped me or if anything had been done to me at all, an exam by a doctor would tell them the truth. Because something like rape couldn't be faked if a physician were involved. She could recognize the change in my behavior and know that something had happened but because of her own personal feelings for Charles and me she had to have her doubts confirmed.

Sky could take no more and stormed out the door still clutching Libby's apron, I don't think he even realized it was in his hand and then maybe he did. The officer that had escorted Charles out of the room returned and whispered into the detectives' ear. I know he told us but I still don't remember his name. He informed us that Charles had given a full confession, and he was calling his lawyer. I felt relieved because now I would not have to say anything, at least for now.

Mother wanted to talk to Charles, but the detective told her it would have to wait. He then asked me if I could show them the tree house.

I showed them where the tree house was. They began to take pictures and pick up things here and there and put them in little plastic bags. I felt like I was on display and that everyone was staring at me. I wanted to disappear. Actually no one was staring or at least trying not to. One Officer, unaware of my nearness to him, told another if it were his daughter he would have killed him by now and it would be a homicide instead of a rape case. He looked up and saw me there and instantly I saw a look that said he wished he could take it back. I guess he misread the look of appreciation on my face. Because his changed into what appeared to be shame. At the same time I was looking for my own mother who had disappeared. Even now with the trauma of the day's events, I did not get mother's support or love. It felt like she was more concerned about proving his innocence than protecting mine. To get away or maybe to hide, I decided to walk and headed toward the waterfall that I could hear a short distance away.

Then Libby came speeding across the field honking her horn and yelling like someone or something was after her. The detective met her and she told him something that made him start yelling for everyone to get back to the house.

The police came in through the front door, but the rest of us entered the house though the kitchen, I saw something that knocked all of the wind out of me. It was as if my breath was solid and someone just walked up and took it away.

Sky and my mother were standing over Charles' body. My mother had a gun in her hand. Libby's gun. The detective checked Charles and found him barely breathing and trying to speak. The detective told him to stay quiet and was about to request an ambulance over his hand radio, when Charles snatched the radio and said that he deserved to die. He passed out and I was sure he was dying. For a moment I thought I saw something in his eyes as he stared at me, but I was never sure. But we all saw the tear roll down his cheek.

The detective called for an airlift and had his partner watch Charles to make sure he kept breathing until help arrived. The officer was checking his pulse and his breathing.

Again I found myself in a room with a man on the floor in a pool of blood. It seems that so much of my life was Deja vu. It's as if there is some toxic entity that wants us to relive the same traumatic events over and over.

The detective demanded to know what happened. Libby said she heard three shots and ran into the kitchen and Charles was lying on the floor with Sky and mother standing over him with the gun in her hand. The detective turned and asked if anyone cared to explain. No one spoke. The detective read them both their rights and had them escorted to a car outside. They never spoke another word, to each other or anyone else the rest of the day. Sky was taken to the Juvenile Detention Center and mother was taken to the Women's Holding Center.

There was this loud sound like a big storm outside, then some men came rushing in the back door and began working on Charles. The things they were saying sounded like a foreign language for as much as I could understand. I did remember some of the words from when mother was in the hospital, some of the nurses use to talk to each other that same way so I figured that it was medical stuff.

Libby was standing over in the corner crying softly and praying. I could not hear her words but I know that's what she was doing because she always said that one should pray when they are scared, and she was. She said pray when someone was sick or dying and I thought surely Charles must be.

I tried hard not to feel relieved about not having to explain any more details about what had happened at the treehouse. But I also felt sad about Charles and that did not make any sense either. I could not understand feeling sad for someone who had done this awful thing to me. But a man had been hurt, possibly dead because of me and I did not want that thought stuck in my head for life. So off to therapy again to deal with more issues in my life brought about by someone else's' problems. First my father and mother, now Charles.

Charles spent four hours in surgery while they removed the bullets and repaired the damage. Libby went to the hospital as his next of kin and because I had no intentions of going home to be interrogated by Ashley, I stayed with Libby. I felt odd and out of place sitting there waiting to find out if he would live or die. I sat holding Libby's hand and thinking I could have stayed right there in the same place all day, if we had not been at the hospital waiting to see if the only family Libby had would live thru the day. We didn't talk we just sat there waiting and watching the people come and go.

Just like before the nurses wanted to have me put somewhere out of earshot, but Libby was not having it. She told the nurses thank you, but no thanks. She wanted to keep me in her eyesight. The nurses were not aware of the day's events and would never understand that Libby felt responsible. Somehow I knew that she felt that it was her fault just as I felt that it was mine.

After his release from the hospital, Charles was sent to prison. Everything was left in Libby's care pretty much as it had always been. Sky and I managed to keep in touch with Libby and having her in my life helped me more than any therapist ever could. Although I healed physically I started to have nightmares again, and was told that they were a psychological response to recent events. I spent a lot of time thinking and worrying about all the things that had happened in our lives and why they had happened. The answers that I came up with did not make me feel better but only confused me more; but I was only eleven years old, and no one was really interested in discussing my feelings so that meant I had to work it out on my own.

I began to think life may be too difficult for people to live and that's why all these strange things keep happening to me and my family. Also, maybe we were bad people and all this was punishment and really meant to happen.

CHAPTER TWELVE..... JUSTICE COMES CALLING

Weeks later Lt Alexander came to give us an update on things. He said that although his lawyer had shown up, Charles refused his services and sent him away. Charles confessed to what he did because he said Libby made him promise to tell the truth and face the consequences of his actions. Lt Alexander spent some time talking to mother in another room and I was never told what they discussed, but when he was leaving he looked at me with very sad eyes as if he wanted to say or do something but he just looked down at the floor and left.

Later that evening I hid in the closet and called Libby. I had to know what was really going on and I knew that Libby would tell me. She told me that the detective told her the hardest part of the whole case was explaining in his report how Charles was shot while in custody. He also wanted to know why I was not treated or in the hospital, why mother did not take me to the hospital.

I found out from Libby all the details. She told me, much later of course, that Sky told her everything and she relayed the story to me. She never said when he told her, but that he wanted to talk about it and would not talk to anyone but her and only when no one was around.

It was told to me that after everyone had left for the tree house, which Sky said to Libby that no man deserved to live after doing something like that. Libby told him it was in the hands of the police now and they would do what was best. But would they, was what she and Sky wanted to know.

Mom went out to the tree house, but after arriving she realized that she needed to confront Charles alone. She arrived at the house via the kitchen door in time to hear that someone else wanted to confront Charles also.

Sky was trying to control the rage in his heart and the fear in his voice as he chastised Charles for his unscrupulous behavior. Charles was trying to justify himself and his behavior, all the while making Sky angrier by the second. The apron was now on the table.

Charles came toward Sky attempting to put his hands on Sky's shoulders hoping to shake some understanding into him. But Sky began to back away, he tripped over the apron ties and fell. The apron fell off the table and the gun landed right in Sky's lap. Charles stopped and stared at Sky, afraid to take another step, for he could see his death in the boy's eyes. As clear as if it were passing before him on a movie screen.

Maria stepped through the door, Sky had the gun trained on Charles' chest. Charles feeling that because he was an adult and this child was once his friend that he could talk him into or out of anything. But this was not the case. Charles took a step toward Sky and reached out to him, Sky assumed that Charles was going to attack him as he had Dee and fired a shot. More out of surprise than anything else but the bullet hit Charles in the upper stomach. The look on Sky's face said that he knew he was in control and that he could do what he wanted, so he raised the gun and aimed at Charles a second time, this time with the determination of a vengeful man and fired the gun. Maria saw what was about to happen and tried to grab the gun away from Sky. But in the struggle the gun went off. Sky fell to the floor and mother grabbed him thinking he had been shot, Libby entered the kitchen and screamed, and mother turned toward Libby and then followed her eyes. She saw Charles lying on the floor holding his stomach.

Sky began to scream at Charles; that it served him right, he deserved to die. Even if Sky was looking at Charles he wasn't seeing Charles. His eyes had a distant stare in them. He wasn't really seeing Charles at all, but past him or maybe through him. Mother did her best to calm him for she was also feeling an old familiar pain. She helped him stand and gain some form of composure, just as the kitchen started to fill with people. Just as my mother and brother were feeling old pains, I too was starting to feel an old familiar fear creeping up on me. That feeling of being closed in and wanting to be outside in the air.

Sky was never quite the same after that. He was always sweet to me and highly protective but changed nonetheless. My mother was angry that I did not make her understand my fear of Charles was real. Ashley was even more standoffish than before. But then she felt it was my fault. She would never speak the words, but with those expressive brown eyes, she never had to.

Because of the situation and the surrounding circumstances there was no formal trial. But once again my family, what was left of it, was ordered to seek professional help. Sky finally stopped going to see the therapist because he felt he was confusing her, more than she was helping him.

Mother continued to see her therapist; and still does. She felt that her life would benefit by the outlet that her trips to Dr. Chase could provide.

I clung to Libby even if it was just by phone. I knew one day I would be old enough to go see her on my own whether mother agreed or not. Once Sky learned that he could trust her, he began to talk to Libby more as well, but only when no one was around to hear.

CHAPTER THIRTEEN.....
NEW AGE SIBLING RIVALRY

Needless to say we grew past that traumatic event in our lives. Sky and I remained close. We continued to feel that it was us versus the rest of the world. Even though there was no longer any threat of physical abuse from father; and mother having her therapy sessions had stopped drinking, there was no closeness among us. As Sky and I grew older we grew closer to each other and further from everyone else including mother. Our only other close connection was to Libby.

With a thoughtful suggestion from Ashley mother put Skylur and I in a private school. Hoping that a structured environment would help us. Neither one of us liked the idea, it felt more like a punishment. We said as much to our mother and because she expected us to behave badly, embarrass her or worse get expelled; she decided to use the one weapon she had, Libby. After getting Libby on board with the idea, she turned Libby loose on me and Sky, needless to say not only did we go but we behaved and did well. We remained uneventfully in a private school, Our Lady of Grace, until high school.

Mother investigated all the local high schools like she was planning a trip for the president, she tried Sky first. Even being behind age wise he made up for it intellectually. Having attended private school those few years made the fact that he was almost a year older than his classmates kind of disappear. By that time mother was comfortable enough to live without

Ashley around to dote on. Ashley, on the other hand, had started dating and only needed an occasional sitter for the girls, knowing Libby was not an option, meant mother was it. Having felt obligated to Ashley for all her help Mother kept the girls whenever Ashley wanted without complaint.

Sky didn't show any interest in sports or other team activities. His favorite hobby was restoring old furniture and reading books about restorations of famous houses and of course, keeping up with me. He seemed to always know where I was, what I was doing and what I was thinking. At times it could be kind of creepy, but when I was in a tight spot it was great to have a big brother that could read my mind. It was also a great help when I wanted to talk and didn't know quite how to start the conversation. We would find a quiet corner and talk about whatever came to mind. For me it was school and classes for him it was the latest restoration project or newest book he had read on the same subject.

It seemed that we were finally getting into a pattern of normality. No late night fights, or tree house episodes jumping out at us. The only time we were of different minds was when I would want to talk about the past. Sky would never be mean to me but he would discourage the conversation as nicely as possible. We would spend our weekends at the library or the Barnes & Noble bookstore because they were close to home and mother did not see any way that anything could happen if we were together and close to home. Those were the only places we both liked and mother would give us money for, so it worked out perfectly. Also, our trips to the library or bookstore on the weekends made it easy to stop and call Libby. I always went first and then Sky, he didn't like for me to listen so I would sit and read whatever new book I had.

For me high school was uneventful for the first two years because I was shy and withdrawn. Then my junior year I felt a little more adventurous, so I joined a few clubs and became more active and a little more social. I even became brave enough to date a little.

Sky was coaxed into sports to keep his reputation from being tainted by the fact that he didn't date or hang out with guys very often. I tried to set him up with some of my friends that were a little older, but he always managed to formulate a believable excuse even though I knew the truth. He would come to the school dances to stand in corners and give my dates very threatening looks if they got too close or held me to tightly when we were dancing.

I had seen glimpses of Sky's temper but never experienced a full blown episode. I knew he had a temper because Libby would occasionally tell him to mind that his temper did not turn him into the one thing he never wanted to become. I never knew what she meant because Sky would not talk to her when I was present but I knew it was important because she told him this often. My junior year and his senior year the reason for Libby's constant reminders made an awful appearance. One that nearly ruined my relationship with my brother forever.

Once, at a school dance, the guy that was supposed to be my date was not happy that I was not comfortable slow dancing with him. I told him I was perfectly ok with him dancing with someone else if he wanted too. He keep asking and I kept saying no and then he decided that I was going to dance whether I wanted to or not. He grabbed my hand and pulled me on the dance floor, when I tried to pull away and leave he grabbed my arms and shook me. He was telling me that I was his date and that I was supposed to dance with him. Sky was a chaperone and when Bradley shook me and I screamed at him to stop, Sky grabbed him from behind, spun him around and punched him in the face. I tried to grab Sky and stop him but one of the female chaperones grabbed me and pulled me away, saying let the males handle it. Somehow I knew that they were not going to be able to help Bradley or stop Sky.

Bradley being a football player grabbed Sky around the waist and tried to throw him to the floor. Sky slammed his forearm into Bradley's back and drove him to floor, he then jumped on him and began punching him over and over in the face. Several of the other guys at the dance were trying to pull him off Bradley, with no success. Even a few of the other football players were attempting to help. Sky just kept punching and I realized that Bradley was not fighting back, in fact he was not moving at all and there was blood everywhere. I got away from the person holding me and ran to

Sky and got right in his face and started talking to him like I use to when I was little and afraid during our parents fights. I grabbed his face and made him look at me, he reached up and shoved me really hard and when I hit the floor and screamed his name everything stopped. The sudden silence was deafening.

The sound of my scream broke something inside Sky and helped to bring him out of the place he had gone to. He immediately jumped up and ran to me and pulled me into his arms and began looking around for someone else to attack to protect me from.

The ambulance was called and Bradley was taken away, just as my father and just as Charles had been. I was scared and shaking, I had never seen Sky act this way and this was something that was more in keeping with the type of man my father was, not Sky. I really did not want to be that close to Sky at that moment but after his recent actions I was afraid to try to move away from him because I was not sure how he might react.

The police came and Sky had to explain his actions and when he was trying to tell the police that hearing me cry triggered something inside him, they did not understand and thought that there was some jealousy or revenge involved and that was why he attacked Bradley in such a viscous manner.

While Sky was talking with the police, I was trying to pull myself together when I saw a face that I recognized enter room. Lt Alexander looked as if he wanted to be anywhere but at a high school dance, but once he saw me and then Sky with blood on his clothes and hands his demeanor changed instantly. The Lt I remembered from years ago came out to the forefront and took over. Something about the storm cloud gray of his eyes made me start to relax a little.

Lt Alexander walked over to the small group off in the corner and once he spoke the dynamics changed and then they all walked outside. I made to follow but he looked at me and shook his head. About 20 minutes later he came, got me and then drove us home.

Lt Alexander spoke to mother on the porch while Sky went to shower and change. I sat there numb and uncertain. A feeling I had grown very familiar with in those last few years. Mother came back in the house about the same time Sky came out the shower. She told us both to go to bed and we would talk later. Sky attempted to apologize for his behavior but mother told him that we would talk later and then walked away. Sky turned and reached for me to hug me and I jumped at his touch, I am not sure why but I did. He just stood there staring at me and I realized what true suffering looked like on the face of someone you love but could not help in any way. Something I realized my brother was very familiar with.

Neither of us went back to school for about a week and when we did, no one said anything about the incident at the dance, at least not that we could hear. We learned that Bradley had a severe concussion and his jaw was broken so badly it had to be wired shut to heal. He would not be back to school this year and probably not play any more football.

During the first two days at home, Sky did not say anything to anyone just sat quietly in his room or outside in an old tire swing that we never used. By day three my fear had passed and all I wanted was for my brother to hug me and tell me things would be okay as always. So I went out to the swing and told him that I was afraid, but instead of reaching for me he simply asked me what I was afraid of.

This was different and I did not like it, but somehow I knew he was waiting for me to tell him that he was what I was afraid of. Although I was at the dance, I wasn't now, so I told him the truth. I was afraid of not being allowed to go back to school because I finally learned to like maybe even love it and I did not want to lose that. He looked up at me and stared as if he were searching for a speck of untruth, a hint of a lie in my face. I made sure there was none to be found and to insure it I took a step closer to him. He stood held open his arms and I ran the last few steps into them.

We were back, back to us against the world and back to what we were before and I could not explain the comfort I felt. I knew it really would be okay at that point and I felt the weight of the last few days leave me.

When Sky and I arrived back at school and we were directed to the principal's office. We were told that Sky would be back on a probationary basis because of the extenuating circumstances and that there was to be no more sports, no more fights and he could not chaperone any more dances. Of course he agreed and that was how the school year ended.

Nana Jones told us that Lt Alexander had something to do with it, she just didn't have any details or proof but she felt strongly about it. Ashley wanted to know why we both had not been expelled, why Sky was not being charged with something and why I was acting as if it was all okay that two boys were fighting over me and one had been seriously injured. I gave no response because it was just like Ashley to assume the worst of us and especially me.

Months later when I was able to talk to Libby, she told me that when she heard about what happened she began praying for all of us, Bradley included. She also told me that Lt Alexander sent her a letter explaining everything because he knew she would be the one that would help us the most. He also told her that he had gone to the principal's house and spoke with him about the events at the dance and about our history. After that we both knew why things had happened the way they did.

Sky graduated from school and went to work. He did not want to go away to college and he didn't want to be away from me. I loved my brother a lot and I was happy to have him around but I did not want him to put his life on hold, simply to protect me.

I think Sky just wanted to be close to me because he worked and made more than enough to live on his own, but he stayed at home until I graduated and started college.

CHAPTER FOURTEEN.....
AND BABY MAKES THREE

All the things I had heard my last year of high school about college were true. I was still not as bold and outgoing as some of my friends, but I managed to snag a date now and then. Even though Sky was not physically present, he remained supportive and understanding, only now over the phone and through the mail. Anything exciting that happened I had to call and tell him about, then I had to call Libby.

Mother knew Sky and I maintained our close connection to Libby and never said anything about us talking to her or driving to visit her, but I always got the feeling that she didn't like it.

I met this guy my senior year; he was sensitive, sexy and painfully shy. He seemed perfect for me because I was the same. We sat next to each other in three classes and during lunches. We talked a lot first then we started to date. Ricardo and I had a lot in common, especially difficult childhoods. The difference was that he would openly talk about his and I would not.

Ricardo told me about his being a lock and key kid and taking care of himself after school and spending weekends hanging out with his mom and all the fun things she would plan for them to do. He said that was her way of making up for his being alone so much during the week, and having to help with homework over the phone. He never mentioned his father and I did not want to ask in fear that he might ask about mine.

His mother Janice worked for an attorney that she often said would never marry because Basil Galbreath was already married to his job. Because her boss worked such long hours Janice often worked late, just so she could be ready and prepared for the next day. Janice really loved her job and she said it was worth it to put in the long hours.

Ric was also very close to his mom and that was something I had no experience with so when I met her for the first time it was uncomfortable for me that they would laugh and tease each other. But Janice was nice and seemed to pick up on my need to go slow in meeting and getting close to people. We spent most of our time together at his house because it was close to campus and his mom was ok with us being together.

We spent so much time together that my mother wanted to meet him. I think she hated him on sight because he was so quiet. She said he was too quiet and he looked very sneaky.

I never told Ric how my mother felt about him, but he figured it out on his own. Besides we were not around mother often enough for it to really matter.

I was curious about his father because he never mentioned him and neither did his mom almost like he was avoided on purpose. On the rare occasions that his father came up, Ric called him Paul and not dad or father. I thought that was odd but did not want to pry.

One Saturday on a picnic in the park I asked about his dad and he became quiet and pensive. He told me he didn't know him and really had no desire too. He told me his father's name was Paul Devereaux, he was an attorney and someone he never wanted to be like. He said his dad came to work at Galbreath, Gray & Hines where his mom worked as a consultant to help with a big case his mom's boss was covering. Paul met Janice and they were very attracted to each other. He never said he was married and was not wearing a ring so Janice felt very special when he asked her out.

They ate lunch together and went out often after work when he was not working late and it did not take long for the relationship to become serious. Ric said his mom fell hard for Paul and he seemed to feel the same about her, so she was very excited when she found out she was pregnant.

The excitement was short lived, because it was around the same time that the big case ended and Paul was preparing to return to where he lived. Because Paul never said anything about their relationship once the case was over Janice began to wonder if the whole thing had been one sided or that she had imagined his feelings for her. So Janice let Paul leave and never told him about the baby.

When Janice's boss found out about the baby he was very angry and upset and Janice thought it was because he would have to be without her while she was out on maternity leave, turns out that was not the case at all.

Shortly after Mr. Galbreath found out about the baby, Janice overheard a loud argument between her boss and someone on the phone. He left early and told her he was taking a few days off and that she could too.

Janice had started to regret having never told Paul about the baby so she decided to go see him and tell him. When she arrived she tried calling him at the number that had been listed for him but no one was home and she was not comfortable leaving a message. When Janice found the address there were two children playing in the yard, but as the taxi pulled up and she got out the children went next door so she assumed that's where they lived.

Janice was nervous so she asked the taxi to wait for her, Ric said his mother told him once that that she never knew why she felt compelled to tell the driver to wait; but was glad in the end that she had.

The woman that answered the door was very pretty and Janice almost turned around and walked away thinking she had the wrong address, that is until Paul walked up behind her and open the door wider asking who was it. He acted as if he had never seen her before and even denied that he had ever met her. Janice told Ric she was in shock and turned around and ran back to her taxi. She went back to the hotel and just sat there numb and lost.

The next week when she went back to work she told her boss that she was resigning and moving back home so that she would have help with her child. He never accepted her resignation and told her she had to stay because he was already spoiled and no one else would put up with him.

Ric said months later before he was born Janice told her boss that she never knew Paul was married and her boss told her he knew and that was why he and Paul had argued months before. He told her he was somewhat responsible for her situation because he had known that Paul was married and figured out later that Paul had lied to him when he said he had told Janice that he was married and that they were just enjoying each other's company nothing more. Paul told Basil that Janice was nice and fun to talk too. He always denied that there was ever anymore to it. So when John had found out about the baby he was angry that Paul had lied to them both.

Janice's boss insisted that anything she or the baby needed that she come to him. He and his wife became Ric's godparents then Basil became more than a boss to his mom but a friend.

Janice never had any further contact with Paul and had no knowledge of whether or not her boss ever told him anything about the baby. The last she heard was when Ric was about five years old that Paul died with an AIDS related illness. She had herself and Ric tested and found that she was HIV positive but she had not passed it on to Ric. Janice insisted that Ric be tested every year until he was about 15 then she finally accepted that he was not at risk.

Janice never appeared sick and only on occasion would she look a little pale and weak, he had assumed it was because she did not go out in the sun much.

Ric said she stayed out of the sun because of her medications and they were close because she had taught him to be happy with every day that they got to be together.

Of course, I never told mother about Janice and her condition, it was also the first time I did not share with Sky but I did talk to Libby and she told me that God has his own reasons for the things that He allows to happen to His children. She did tell me that I should be careful.

Mother continued to make little negative comments about Ric, she said that he was not the type of man she wanted for me. She told me that I should be careful that he did not make me regret having ever met him. I guess what hurt the most was that Libby agreed with mother. Although,

Libby's reasons were different, her feelings were still the same. All these years of disagreeing on everything including why they disagreed, they picked this time to agree. I told Ric about it and he said he understood how much Libby meant to me and that he would respect whatever decision I made. So Ric and I consented to spending time away from each other. I even agreed that we should date other people.

We tried but neither one of us was really interested in anyone else. So to keep down confusion at home we pretended to go out with other people. I mostly went to visit Sky and he stayed at home. When that got old we began dating again but under the disguise of double dates. Near the end of the semester we started spending more time alone together to avoid the cold stares from my mother.

Eventually, with one thing leading to another we began sleeping together. Either at his house or at mine, whichever place where no one was at home. I found sex to be difficult at first, naturally with my past as it had been. But Ricardo was very understanding and gentle. I never told him about my past, I could not find the right words or the right time. I guess I really didn't see a need, he was always gentle and very slow. He never pushed, he gave me all the time I needed to make up my mind that I was ready for an intimate relationship. For that I was grateful, even if Libby and my mother felt he was wrong for me. I don't think any other man would have been as easygoing and gentle with me. Although he was kind and took his time and always went slow with me, I never had the nerve to tell him it was not the pleasure to me he said it would be once I got use to it. But because it made him smile and he would kiss me softly and always hold me so close afterwards, I told myself it was worth it. Of course this was also something that never made it into my letters or calls to either Sky or Libby. That bothered me because I had never not shared anything with Sky and I could talk to Libby about most anything, somehow my having sex with Ric never got discussed. But I felt Libby knew anyway.

Halfway through the summer break I woke up very sick one morning. After a trip to the doctor that I did not need to know what was wrong mother called Ric. When he arrived he looked very concerned. Mother was very brief; she told him I was pregnant and she wanted to know what his intentions were. Ric gave mother a look of sheer horror because we had discussed marriage and knew we were not ready.

I think we were both afraid of marriage because of the way things were with our parents. Neither set gave us the best examples to go by. I had talked with Libby and she felt that the decision we made would be best for us and that we should focus on what would be best for the baby.

After listening to my mother express her feelings about the situation and about Ric, we talked alone for a while, then he left. I told mother that we were not going to get married because we were not ready. She was not happy with this at all. She told me that although she did not like Ric, she felt that not getting married was a mistake, but I would have to live with whatever choice I made.

I explained that we both would be working in a few weeks and would be able to take care of the baby and ourselves. Thank God that our programs of study offered job placement so we didn't have that to worry about finding jobs.

I was more afraid of Libby's reaction than my mother's. Libby's presence in my life was what had kept me going thru the worst possible times and I could not imagine being without her. Libby was very quiet when I told her about the baby. She listened to me and did not say much and it frightened me because she always had something to say. After a while I stopped talking and sat there holding the phone so tight I heard the plastic creaking under the abusive grip of my fingers. Finally I called her name and Libby answered me, she said that she was praying for us all because she felt that this pregnancy could be a good thing or a bad thing only God knew which. We talked some more then I hung up and had to lay down because of the pounding headache I had given myself worrying.

Sky did not want mom to know it but he was happy for me. Ric and I kept seeing each other and making plans for our lives after graduation from college. It took a while getting use to the idea of being parents but we were also very excited.

Sky spent as much time with me as possible. Even though we were no longer the frightened little children we once were, we still found much comfort in talking to each other versus other people. We also chose each other's company more so than the friends and family we had acquired. Ashley said once that we were like a set of twins joined at the hip. Sky never made any comments but I always felt that he never cared for Ashley and was happy when she was not around as often.

When the baby began moving and kicking it seemed natural that I would call Sky and then Libby. Ric would smile and say things like, good that means the baby is healthy and strong. Sky would rub my belly and talk to the baby and try to get it to move around more. Libby constantly fed me, it was always you need to eat. You need to gain a few pounds. Left up to Libby I would have gained 50 lbs. and she would have been great with it. I wanted to be at home in my own place those last few weeks before the baby came but Libby felt that I needed to have someone with me, so I stayed at the ranch with her. It was comfortable being with Libby, like always she would talk to me about life and things that would have me in deep thought even hours later when I was in bed. I talked to Ric on the phone several times a day and he would come and visit 2 or 3 times a week.

I had always hoped that Ric and Sky would become friends but there was not enough common ground. Outside of their attachment to me they had nothing in common and most often would not even attempt conversation.

Joshua was born as beautiful as I knew he would be. Ric stayed with me the entire time I was in labor. Sky and Libby took turns pacing in the waiting room. Sky fussing about how long it was taking and Libby insisting that they pray for the health and safety of me and the baby. Mother arrived about an hour before the baby came and just sat quietly immersed in her own thoughts. She had no comments or conversation for anyone, not even me.

I was in labor a long time and we were not sure if Libby was going to survive it. Everyone came through it fine and Josh was a very healthy baby and Libby fell in love with him on sight. Ric wanted to name the baby after him but mother would not hear of it. But we were still happy. I thought Ricardo was the perfect father. He stayed at the hospital with me and took care of both of us. Changing diapers, feeding Josh, keeping me company and getting me food when the hospital food was not what I wanted. He was focused on nothing but me and Josh and it was great. I started to feel that my mother was wrong about him and I was going to find a way to bring it up in conversation and let her know that things did not happen how she thought they would.

Ric helped me get settled at home when Josh was about a month old. I felt it was time to go home, of course Libby disagreed but she understood my need to try things on my own and supported me as always. Mother felt that it was time for me to grow up and stop depending on Libby so much but with her it was because she felt Libby was an intrusion and did not offer any true value. I guess mother would always harbor some anger for Libby, and we all knew why. Ric and Sky would bring toys and other things for the baby to the house every chance they got.

We had planned to move out as soon as Josh was about six months old. By then I would be back at work and strong enough to handle a job and Josh on my own, with Ric's help. Things went great for the first three or four months then it started to fall apart. Ric began to change. He was acting differently towards the baby and me.

Libby insisted that we have a christening for Josh and it seemed that Sky and I were the only ones that didn't have a problem with it. Mother thought it was a ridiculous idea stating that nothing about the whole situation was appropriate and she did not see a need. Ric was uncomfortable with it, but he had become uncomfortable with everything by that time. Janice thought we should wait until Ric and I were married. I knew that would not be happening anytime soon so, I did not want to wait for that and said so. In the end Libby got her way. The christening happened at the ranch because no one could agree on a church. Mother and Ashley were late, so that caused an argument between her and Nana Jones. Aunt Alice got lost and Sky had to go find her. Ric never showed up so Sky happily stood in his place.

Later Libby pulled me aside and told me this was one of the reasons she had agreed with mother about him, she did not feel he would be dependable and strong enough to deal with all that life would bring. He called later that evening to say he had gotten tied up at work and lost track of time. Ric said he was sorry and he tried talking about other stuff but I was not in the mood for a conversation with him and told him so and got off the phone. I walked into the kitchen to find Sky and Aunt Alice talking. I walked in just as she was telling Sky that Ric was going to be very sorry the next time he ran into Libby. She said that Libby was going to be after him like an electric feather duster after dust bunnies on roller skates. Sky and I both laughed for a while behind that one, so did Libby. But we all knew Aunt Alice was right.

Ric and I had decided that we were still not ready for marriage and at this point I must say that I am glad we did. Ric came to see me a few weeks after the christening and told me he had found a better job traveling on the road with a man he had met while we were in school. He said he wanted us to discuss his traveling, but the entire time we sat talking; I felt that his decision to leave was already made. I knew that my feelings were true when Ric suggested I get a post office box so that when I finally did move Ric would still know how to find me. He said that he would call me in few days he still had some thinking to do. He left two weeks later.

I started getting these checks in the mail about two weeks after that. I never got a letter, but he did tell me before he left that he would be very busy for the first month or so.

Our relationship ended as expected, not that I wanted it to end but everyone had said that it would so I guess I knew it. After about two months I moved into a two-bedroom cottage not too far from my mom. I did not hear from Ric except for the routine checks in the mail.

My job and my son kept me busy, so after a while I didn't have time to think about Ric. I worked in a stockbroker's office as an apprentice and it was great. The apprentice program was two years long. There was so much to learn I didn't think I could learn it all in two years, but everyone told me I would be fine because I caught on fast. I met and worked with a lot of interesting people. They all seemed very nice and always willing to help me if I needed it.

But the one thing I needed help with no one would be able to help me with, that was trying to decide where to go with my personal life. Josh was almost eighteen months old and I was beginning to wonder if I would ever see Ric again. Maybe these thoughts were brought on by loneliness and a need for companionship or maybe just the need to talk to someone that knew more than fifteen words.

I found myself looking at people differently than I had before, especially male people. One person in particular. But because he was much older than my mere twenty-three and most importantly, married; I kept my distance.

CHAPTER FIFTEEN.....
A FRIENDSHIP BEGINS

After my two-year apprenticeship was complete, the firm was offering permanent work to some of the people in my original group that had stayed the entire two years and been productive. I was offered an opportunity for a permanent position. Of course I took it. But I was not aware that my position would put me in "his" office.

Mr. Giovanni Armando Smith, II. He was six feet four inches of sheer heaven. Big soft green eyes with a hint of gray, which reminded me of a pair that seemed to stare out at me from the corners of my mind. Broad shoulders that seem to go on forever. Big strong arms that promised the protection that only a father could provide. Gentle hands that offered a baby's touch with long fingers that ended in well-manicured but masculine nails. He spoke fluent French, which was his father's native tongue. He had a mane of long thick black hair, which was kept in control in the form of a ponytail. He had a strong jawline that ended in an oval shaped face, these and other features gave one the distinct impression of Indian heritage. Maybe his mother. Whichever parent gave him whichever features, it did not matter because he was a masterpiece.

I would catch glimpses of him throughout the day and store them up for later to daydream. He always had a ready smile and a pat on the back for those who needed it to keep them going. I was so fascinated by him that I would hide in the foyer or around corners just to sneak a peek at him.

Sometimes just knowing we were in the same office was just what it took to get me up and out of bed.

Everyone called him AJ, except me, at his request. He was a perfect gentleman at all times. He had this easygoing style that made everyone relaxed and comfortable whenever he was around. Everyone in his office worked as a team. That was his first rule. It was also his motto that you saw on a plaque on the wall in his office; "teamwork produces great work".

We often worked late to give our clients our best. This was always done under his guidance and direction. I noticed that he was always at the office, no matter how early or how late we were there, he was there too.

Erica Cason was the office bitch. Every office had one and she was our burden to bear. You know the type, drop dead good looks with a figure that didn't look a day over twenty-five. I think she hated me from the day I got assigned to that office. I could never figure out what I could have done to make her act the way she did, but I very quickly realized I was not the only one in the office that had won her hatred. There were three of us and yes we were all females, jealousy I doubt very seriously; but one can never be sure.

Several times I considered requesting a transfer to get away from her. But after a letter from Libby, with her motherly wisdom along with continued encouragement to pray for guidance, I would always abandon the idea.

As always Libby remained my source of encouragement and emotional support. I talked to her at least once a week, when I needed to vent things that were difficult to say I would write her letters. Libby was my proverbial diary and the ranch was and always would be a place of solace for me. Charles' had left everything in Libby's capable hands. His attorney had agreed because he had never married, had no children and no other family and no one knew the running of the place as well as Libby.

I wrote to Libby about AJ and how handsome he was and I could always imagine her wonderful laugh. I still feel to this day that some of my letters to Libby were childish but Libby swore that they brought a smile to her face, and brightened her day.

Once we had an office party to celebrate some major event in the life of the ever popular, and hated by all. Of course, Ms. Cason. I took a picture of AJ. I wrote Libby and told her I would bring it with me on my next visit to the ranch. I told her I could not bear to part with it long enough to send it through the mail. She called the next day to tell me she understood that I might dry up and blow away without it.

My first real encounter with AJ came about because I had to leave work early because Josh was ill; so I decided to come in early the next day to catch up on the work I had missed. AJ was already there, at six in the morning; hair loose and wild, face unshaved and looking just as surprised as I felt. It was then that I learned the real truth behind his being the first person in and the last one out. He was sleeping on the sofa in his office.

My first thought was of him and Erica on that sofa, unfair I know but couldn't help it. It just popped into my head. Libby was sure to get me for that one. I felt sorry for him, so I offered to share my breakfast. He gladly accepted. Somehow I knew at that point that I would not get any work done, not this morning anyway. He shaved and dressed and I made coffee, I drank tea because Libby would not approve of my drinking coffee. We shared my bacon and egg sandwich and talked for what seemed like hours.

I was surprised at how easy it was to talk to him, after all he was my boss. He was very interested in the lives of the people that worked for and with him. He was also a great listener and spoke to me as if we had been friends for ever and that made me feel special. No one, especially a man, had just sat and talked with me about everything and nothing. At least not since Ricardo. That thought brought me some sadness and was a painful reminder of what my life was really like. Lonely except for Josh.

I was talking to him about my college years leaving out Ric, of course. Then I noticed that he was sitting there simply staring at me or maybe not seeing me at all. This made me think I was boring him so I stopped talking and just sat quietly. I guess he thought my silence meant it was his turn to speak and he had missed some unspoken cue. He started talking but what he was saying didn't go along with what we had been talking about, so again I just sat quietly. I realized that the conversation had turned very personal and I was not sure how to handle it. I did not want my fantasy of him ruined by finding out that he was not the perfect man I thought him to be.

But when I stopped wandering along in my own thoughts and started to really listen to what he was saying I learned a lot of things that did change my thoughts of him but not in the manner I was expecting.

He told me all about his non-existent home life. How he wanted children and his wife wanted her career. So basically they were on the outs, the usual story. He made the mistake of asking me about myself and whether or not I wanted children, which opened up the can of worms I had kept a lid on all this time. So that's when it all came out, my story about Ric and Josh and everything. When I finally stopped talking it dawned on me how much I had told him and who I was actually talking too. I sat there staring at the floor mortified. I could not believe I had actually let out all those thoughts and to someone other than Libby or Sky, embarrassed was an understatement to say the least. I was too afraid to look up at his face because of what I expected to see.

He was very understanding and also very interested in my life and my son. Something he wanted very badly.

We talked about everything under the sun. I kept thinking I can't wait to tell Libby about this. He was great to talk to, I could not believe how much better I felt and I told him so. He told me that the conversation had been good for him too. Finally I had to go to the ladies room, so I excused myself.

Erica came in while I was gone, I came out just in time to hear her tell him that she had brought breakfast. He told her thanks but no thanks he had already had his. I felt a small victory at this comment when I saw the look on her face. I came out just in time to get caught in the elevator crowd coming into work so Erica never saw me, or suspected I was there before her.

I started on my work for the day, putting off yesterday's until later. At that moment the hairs on my neck began this offbeat little dance as if something awful and dangerous were coming up behind me. I looked up and saw Erica standing over my shoulder. She was requesting yesterday's reports to give to AJ. I was instantly reminded that she was his assistant and all reports went through her, proofing she called it. I told her they were incomplete because I had left early due to my child being ill. She was about to go into one of her lectures about letting one's personal life interfere with one's professional life, when AJ walked up and said it was okay. He said with a smile directed at me that some things were more important than our jobs and business. He winked at me and told me to come in early or take it home and finish it. Erica was livid, he had never interfered in that manner before. So this was a shock to her ego as well as her self-imposed authority. AJ also had rules about micromanaging and undermining persons he placed in authority, so you can imagine Erica was more than a little bemused. It was also his rule that one kept their personal and professional lives separate, and after having spent several hours talking to him I knew why. This was why he had on more than one occasion verbally expressed a severe dislike for work being done at home.

Erica wanted to demand an explanation but thought better of it and decided to follow him and confront him privately in his office. Everyone in the office was staring at me, I felt beautiful like I was on a cloud. I got up and floated off to the copy machine. I knew I would pay for it later but for right now I was sinfully happy.

Most of the people in our office including me, thought that Erica and AJ were having an affair but now I was not so sure. Maybe Erica was just his assistant in the office and that was all there was to it.

Several people had told me that Erica was hoping AJ and his wife would get a divorce, then she would have an opportunity to be with him. Now I was sure that Erica was waiting for something to happen, but I still did not know what. If AJ were sleeping on the couch in his office and Erica knew it and nothing had happened between them then maybe the things I was hearing was simply office gossip or just ugly rumors. Either way, after having spent that morning talking to him and him being as open as he had been I could not imagine him and Erica being involved and tried hard to erase everything connected to that thought from my mind.

I also knew that Libby would have a lot to say about thinking things like that about people without proof. She would say that is akin to judging someone and then as always she would remind me what the bible said about judging others. So I decided to take Libby's route and pray for us all. AJ, because he really needed God to heal his heart, Erica, because she needed God to fix her all the way around and me, because I knew that I needed God's help with my loneliness.

Things got a little hairy for the next few days, the rest of the week actually.

CHAPTER SIXTEEN.....
ERICA'S DAY IN THE SUN

Erica took every opportunity that AJ was out of earshot or the office to criticize, antagonize or belittle me. She would criticize my work for little things that no one else would notice. But all of this was done when AJ was not around to hear her. Everyone in the office felt sorry for me but did not dare say anything. She had fired people before for a lot less. Some say she even fired or would not hire women she thought too attractive and might have caught AJ's attention.

That Friday was the last straw. I was daydreaming about something and made a mistake on a financial report due in that day. As always lately, Erica was standing over my shoulder reviewing my work. Low and behold she caught it. She stood there at my desk yelling and screaming about the embarrassment that I could have caused AJ with my stupid mistake. She began by telling me that I was supposed to be a professional and that lately my work was close to that of a retarded child. Then she made a crack that maybe I would do better if I let my illegitimate son do my work for me, that it couldn't make my work look any worse. At that point I stood up about to slap her face and call her a jealous bitch and a few other things I had been thinking of, that Libby would have me praying for forgiveness for on Sunday. But as I got to my feet Erica must have realized that she had gone too far, because she was staring at my face and backing away from me like she had poked a snake that was not dead. She backed right into AJ. He grabbed her by the arm and told her that this time she had gone too far. He had been standing there listening. No one dared interrupt Erica to tell her anything, and I had not seen him walk in the office. He walked her half dragging her into his office. I stood there fuming because I didn't get to say what was on my mind, more so than the fact that she had insulted my child and completely humiliated me in front of the entire office. All I could do was head to the bathroom and scream. I did just that and cried some too, but with my face in a towel sitting in a closed stall, just in case someone else came in behind me. I sat there a few minutes and then headed back to my desk. I had to try to work, I was behind enough already so leaving was not an option. I ended up just sitting there doing what everyone else was doing, listening.

After about twenty minutes with nothing coming from the office but muffled voices, Erica came out red-faced and crying. She walked up to me and mumbled something of an apology and ran to the elevators. AJ came out and told everyone to take the rest of the day off and requested that I come to his office.

He met me at the door and told me he wanted to apologize for Erica's behavior. He began this long string of statements about Erica not being the woman he once thought her to be. That she had been long overdue for some type of reprimand for her treatment of the staff. He seemed more upset than I was. I told him it was okay that I had calmed down and I could deal with Erica. I could tell there was something other than the incident with Erica and me that had him upset.

He sort of dropped in his chair and began to stare across the desk at me as if there was something he wanted to say to me but was not sure how to bring up. I told him that I appreciated his saving me from embarrassing myself and losing my job by getting into a physical altercation with Erica. I told him I knew he was upset by her behavior but it did not require that sad look on his face or in his eyes. I waited a few moments to see if he would speak, when he was not forthcoming with whatever was behind the tortured expression, I told him thank you again and stood to leave. He asked me to stay but still said nothing just continued to sit there with that hurt animal look in his eyes. I could tell he needed more than wanted to talk, but he did not know how to get started. So I put him out of his misery and asked what was behind the long face. He asked how much time did I have. I told him considering the fact that he had just given me the day off, I had plenty of time and to go ahead and spill the beans. He told me that he had been hearing reports of Erica's abuse and ill treatment of the staff but was never sure how much was truth and how much was rumor. Something about that statement caught my attention but I could not stop and evaluate it at the moment. I asked him if he suspected why not simply ask, again that little feeling of Deja vu.

AJ said that he had known Erica since they were teenagers and had thought of her as a little sister. He told me how their fathers had been introduced by some of their business partners and Mr. Smith had advised Erica's father on some business investments and that lead to them working together a lot over the years. Because Erica was always after following her father everywhere he would let her go with him, he and Erica had been kind of thrown together and he just took it upon himself to look after her.

AJ started by saying that his mother had warned him many times that Erica expected more because she had been groomed by her mother to do so. Elyssa, Erica's mother, always thought they would make the perfect couple and had voiced it many times even to him. Mrs. Smith told him that Erica was not the type of woman he needed in his life because she was too much her mothers' creature. He did not think either his mom or Erica's were really serious so he paid neither any mind. By the time he left for college it was pretty obvious that he had been wrong in ignoring the warnings.

Because his father and Erica's father were always working and not paying much attention to what was going on with the women, neither was aware of all the plotting going on. Tatianna made it a point to constantly remind Elyssa that Vanni (her pet name for her son) was older than Erica and not romantically interested in her. Elyssa did not agree and told Erica that any man could be won if she really wanted him, so she continued to encourage Erica to pursue AJ.

In the end AJ resolved the whole matter. AJ came home for the holiday season and brought a young lady with him, Leslie. Someone he had been seeing for a while and had decided she was the woman for him. Of course, Erica and Elyssa tried to scare Leslie away and make her think that she was being used to make Erica jealous and that AJ had no real interest in her. But what they did not know was that AJ had already proposed to Leslie and she had accepted.

They were going to make the announcement at the New Year's Eve Ball that his parents gave every year. Needless to say Leslie was not concerned with the two plotting females her only concern was AJ.

So while Erica and Elyssa continued to play games, Leslie just graciously ignored them both. Elyssa and Erica were late arriving to the ball because Erica's father had been late arriving home. AJ said he would never forget the look on Erica's face when she walked in as Giovanni Sr. made the announcement that AJ would be marrying Leslie in the spring with both his parent's blessing.

AJ said that Erica and Elyssa did not attend his wedding but sent him and Leslie a nice gift. He did not see Erica for a few years and when he did, it was during a family party and she said she was looking for a job. AJ said out of respect for her father, he hired her and that was the end of it. AJ did also say his partner Geoffrey never really cared for Erica and was always excusing her from meetings and asking AJ why he tolerated her. AJ admitted that by the time he started to notice that there might be a real problem, he was having problems at home so that dominated his focus, until now.

He sat there and looked at me for a second, really looked at me as if he was searching for something to indicate to him if I was really interested or just being polite. I guess he found his answer, because he said hang on. He called the Deli next door, where we all ate lunch every day, and ordered some lunch. He told me if he was going to bore me to death the least he could do was feed me. I found this kind of funny and I smiled. Something told me that the subject matter would not be so funny, that he was trying to hide his pain behind his humor.

He came around the desk and sat beside me. He told me that he felt that he could tell me anything, I assured him that he could.

He stood up, staring out the window as if he were wishing he were somewhere else. I was trying to decide if maybe I should just leave. Before I could make a decision, he started to walk over to a door. He opened the door and I realized it was a closet. I started to feel that my problems were minimal and unimportant. There were blankets and pillows on the shelves. He had shirts, suits, ties and shoes as well. My concern for his welfare and his feelings increased, I also felt very sorry for him. I began to realize that his problems with his wife had existed for longer than I had initially assumed. This also cleared up my speculation about him and Erica. There was no way he would be living out of his office closet if he and she had something going on. All of a sudden I felt that I owed him an apology for having even let those rumors take hold in my mind even long enough to think twice about them. But I said nothing just sat there and watched him silently berating myself in advance before Libby did, for my thoughts.

He pulled out a blanket and spread it out on the floor. An old familiar fear started to creep up my spine. My palms began to sweat when he removed his tie and roll up his sleeves. I stood up and prepared to run or fight as he opened his two top buttons.

I relaxed a hair when he stopped fidgeting with his shirt. There was a knock at the door, and I nearly jumped across the room. The delivery person gave him a large wicker basket and then seemed to just disappear.

He sat everything on the floor and through my cloud of fear reality clicked in that we were having an indoor picnic. He helped me to the floor and made a comment about my being so tense, that I should relax more. He mentioned something about my reminding him to teach me some relaxation techniques he had learned from his mentor. I knew then that he had just become mine.

The food smelled wonderful, he was silent as he opened the containers. Taking the kind of care used for fine china not paper boxes. When he had everything opened he went about explaining what it all was and how to eat it, giving background information on it like he was teaching me a new investment strategy.

He started to speak about his wife as if he were still talking about the food so I almost didn't catch the change of subject matter. He'd found out three days ago that Leslie had been having an affair. She did not say whether or not she was in love with the man but she had said that it had been going on for two years, I think that speaks for itself. He went on talking and I sat there listening not sure what to say and glad he didn't ask me to say anything. When he stopped speaking, more so to himself than to me, he looked up and I saw the tears in his eyes.

Here was this big strong man crying in front of me. I went to wipe away the tears, and I got pastry cream all over his face. We both laughed hysterically, because the more I wiped the more cream I got on him. He reminded me of Josh when he was hurt and wanted me to kiss it and make it better. Naturally I could not kiss this man, as much as I wanted to, but the cream on his face had the same effect.

We got him cleaned up and talked some more. I don't remember taking my shoes off and lying down on the blanket like a schoolgirl with my feet in the air, but it felt wonderful to be relaxed and have someone to talk to and listen to. He took off his shoes and lay down and we began to tell each other funny stories and jokes it felt like we were old friends that had known each other forever.

After a while we both wanted to go to the little peoples' room, so we took a break. I used his private bathroom and he used the one in the lobby for the employees. While he was gone I noticed that instead of his wife on his desk he had a picture of two older women. He came in as I was looking and told me they were his aunt and his mother. I felt like I was prying into his private life. Never mind all the private things he had told me thus far. He said that he wanted a picture of his father on his desk but, his father told him that it was not very masculine.

He walked up to me and stood very close looking down at me. I didn't know what to say or do, so I pretended to be totally engrossed by the photo I held. He reached out and touched my hair, while he stood there fondling my tresses he began to tell me that he had thought about me a lot since our "breakfast" on mornings past. He told me that he wanted to spend more time with me but he didn't want to make things uncomfortable for me.

We talked more about his home life and I got the feeling he was beating around the bush about what he really wanted to say. He asked me how I would feel about us being friends and talking occasionally until he could work things out at home (if that was possible). He told me that I didn't have to go any further than I wanted or felt comfortable with. I told him to let me think about it. Because I could not look him in the eyes I stared at the carpet, mainly because I did not want him to see the truth in mine.

He gave me a ride to the sitters and wanted to wait and take me home but I came up with an excuse and said thanks but no thanks. He asked if he could call me later and I told him I would like that, but only if he promised to find himself a suitable place to sleep.

That night after Josh was in bed, and I had made my weekly call to Libby; AJ called. We talked about this and that nothing really important. But I could hear something in his voice and he kept avoiding the issue. After about an hour we hung up. I misdialed twice trying to call Libby as promised. She and I talked for a while then hung up. I went to bed that night feeling too excited to sleep but the stress of my confrontation with Erica and the rest of the day put me to sleep before my head hit the pillow.

CHAPTER SEVENTEEN.....
A NEW BEGINNING

I awoke that Saturday feeling new and revived. Josh and I went to the park and the ice cream shop, his two favorite things, and had a long talk about what else to do that day.

I felt like I had earned a day of splurging so I went shopping, wreaking havoc on my budget but it was worth it. AJ was the most prominent man I had ever met, and he was interested in me.

I felt on top of the world. I did not buy any of the conservative type clothes I usually wore, I bought fashions that would show and compliment my greatest asset my legs. Which I usually kept hidden under what Erica called frumpy frocks. I was also thinking of hairstyles that would complement my new wardrobe, styles with my hair down. AJ seemed to prefer my long tresses to Erica's short cut. I remember him saying something about a woman's hair being a major part of her femininity. But I was going to try him out first by wearing it down once and watching his reaction.

My euphoria was short lived for Ricardo called later that afternoon. Ric started talking the minute I said hello and was nonstop from that point on. It was like he had to rush to get everything out before I hung up or stopped listening. He was telling me that he was wrong for his behavior and that he wanted to make things right again. He told me had a great new job that was stationary, that he could take better care of me and Josh and I would not have to work. He also wanted us to get married as planned. I felt trapped; trapped between what I thought was right and what I really wanted.

It made me angry. I felt like Ric somehow knew about AJ and my feelings and was purposely showing up now to ruin everything. I sat arguing with myself that none of what I was thinking and feeling made any sense. AJ was married and had expressed interest because I was there and so desperate for his attention that he talked to me because he needed to talk to someone. But my heart would not accept the reasons my mind was offering. So I decided to really listen to Ric and put my thoughts of AJ and my own personal desires away just for a time. After all, I had a child to think about and as a mother I had to do what was best for him.

Even though I felt I might be given a chance to be with a truly wonderful man, but I did not want to deny Josh a chance to be with his father. What was I going to do? I called Libby. She always spoke from the heart but with common sense. She told me I was counting my chickens before they hatched with AJ. I did not agree but out of love and respect for her I did not say so, although I am sure she knew it anyway.

She told me that I must think about more than my own happiness, which I had to think first and foremost about my son. I sat there and thought about my baby and got up and went to his room. He lay there sleeping very peacefully, taking his afternoon nap. A nap I usually took with him on weekends but not today, there would not be any sleep for me until this situation was handled and put to rest.

Ric told me he would be over at four so we could talk face to face. Talking was never something he wanted to do when I needed him to; now that I was over him and had no need for his conversation he seemed to be overflowing with it. I was still deep in thought and searching for answers when Josh awoke from his nap.

I tried to explain to him that his daddy was coming over, that he wanted us to be a family. As if he knew the confusion in my mind, he asked what I wanted and waited patiently for an answer. I tried to explain to him that there was a time when his daddy's proposal would have made me very happy, but not now. Then I regretted telling my true feelings to such a small child who could not possibly understand especially since I didn't. I was not even sure why I was trying to explain it at all, but something in me said I had to try.

I prayed that my feelings would not confuse him, understanding more than I gave him credit for; Josh climbed up in my lap with a picture of his father we had taken in college pointed to it and strongly said, "No Daddy".

I thought maybe he had misunderstood what I was trying to tell him but I really was not sure how to explain this to a three and a half-year-old child. Josh just kept repeating that same phrase almost as if he knew what I was feeling. I held Josh in my lap to calm him and began to think about his father. I thought that Ric had loved me once but I was not sure about now, Ric had promised to always provide for us and he had kept his promise. But money and love were not the same thing.

His Daddy had been religious about those checks every two weeks, but not once did he call or come to visit. If not me at least Josh. As I sat there with Josh on my lap I thought about the fact that even if I had wanted to write Ric or send him pictures of Josh I couldn't because he never sent one letter with a return address. I had finally come to the conclusion that maybe that was the way he wanted it, and let the matter go. I had not given much thought to it any more since then.

Josh was asleep again so I put him down, then as if he somehow knew I needed a friend AJ called and was very excited. He asked if he could take me to dinner so that we could talk, I told him I needed to think about it. The truth of the matter was as much as I was flattered by the invitation and wanted to go, I knew AJ was a married man. Even if it wasn't much of a marriage, legally he was. I also knew Libby would not approve and she, and her opinion, meant much more than I could ever make anyone understand. He told me he had great news, something I needed right now, and that I was the first to know. Leslie wanted a divorce and he was going to gladly give her what she wanted. I asked why that was such good news, he told me that a very special woman had come into his life and he wanted to give her as much of his time as he could.

He said he felt that she could give him the kind of love he deserved and he could do the same for her. My heart sank in my lap, once again

Libby had been right. I had to know, I asked if it was anyone that I knew, very happily he said yes and no one knows her better than you do. Then I became really confused. I guess he sensed my confusion and AJ told me that I was on his mind a lot and that his wife wanting a divorce could not have happened at a better time in his life. He said that our conversations were what got him through the night and that our working so closely made the days more tolerable. That spending more time with my son and me was what he wanted most right now. Now that he was going to be free of Leslie there would be nothing to stand in the way.

I didn't want to bring it up but I had to know the truth, I asked him about his feelings for Erica. He said there were none. Then he paused for a moment as if there was more he needed to say.

He said he and Erica were childhood friends because their parents had been business partners. That although she had become like a little sister to him, she wanted more than he was willing to give. When he had run into her later after college he gave her a job, which was the extent of their relationship if you wanted to call it that at all. I wanted to believe him so much it hurt, but I had trusted a man before. I started to think about some of the things I had learned about my parent's relationship and did not want my life to be like theirs. I would never allow Josh to go thru what Sky and I had. No matter what my mother said, I could never love anyone enough to put my son through that. Ric had never given me reason to think he may be abusive to me or Josh, but he did have a temper and that made me think anything was possible. Ric had been rather hostile in the end because he just wanted to be free of both of us.

But that was then and this was now. AJ seemed to sense my hesitation, and he told me that he gathered from our talks that my past had been painful. But then I thought so had his, nine years of marriage to a woman that might not have ever loved you. He told me that he knew that what had happened with Ric had hurt me a great deal but that I had to try to get past that. The statement was very familiar, Libby, had told me that years ago and I had told him that about his wife. I was going to try to do just that, I decided to have dinner with him that night.

No, I was not planning to have my cake and eat it too because no matter what happened between AJ and me I was not going to marry Ric anyway, he had hurt me before and I was afraid to trust him again.

I owed it to myself and to AJ to find out what his intentions were. Besides there was no love in my heart for Ric anymore. I would always care about him, for he was my first love. But I knew that was not enough to sustain a marriage.

Just imagining us married frightened me because it reminded me too much of my parents, not that I would ever tolerate him hitting Josh, or me but I could not let Josh endure what I had.

When Ric arrived I told him I could not marry him that my feelings were not the same as he said his were. I told him he could not possibly expect me to continue to love him after all that time without even knowing when or if I would ever see him again.

We talked briefly and he said he did not think it was a good idea for him to see Josh, that Josh would not know him anyway. That things were better left alone between him and Josh. He left promising that he would write Josh a letter and try to explain, somehow I didn't think he would.

When Ric left I sat wondering if I had done the right thing for everyone or just for me. I would soon find out, if things did not work out as I had hoped then I would have gained some experience and lost nothing except some time. Maybe. I could not spend the rest of my life wondering what might have happened if I had given AJ a chance.

Then I remembered the dinner date. That meant I had to find a sitter for Josh. The woman next door had a teenage daughter that would sit for me on occasion for extra money, but this was very short notice.

Angela was glad to keep Josh, she told me that it was about time I got out and had some fun. She said she and her boyfriend had broken up and she would make him jealous by going out with another "man".

Her and Josh would go see the new cartoon movie. She came over to dress Josh and pack an overnight bag for him so that I would have more time. I was very grateful to her for helping out, she said Josh was great company and very cute, this I knew.

CHAPTER EIGHTEEN.....
ERICA'S JUST DESSERTS

AJ was there promptly at eight-thirty, I was still trying to decide what to wear. After letting him in and introducing herself and Josh, Angela poked her head in my room and told me he was wearing jeans and loafers without socks. Problem solved, I put on the same thing.

When I was ready to leave, I stepped in the room with AJ, did a little turn and asked if everything was okay; he told me almost. A million and one things went through my mind, I asked could it be fixed. He told me very quickly and very easily, I stood there staring and very afraid of what he might say or do. He stepped behind me and took my hair down and tossed it a little, and then walked back in front of me and tilted my head up and whispered, "Perfect". I was thinking two hours to get it just right and he had destroyed it in two seconds. But when he came around to face me I was all smiles, because now I knew he liked it down. And that's how it would be.

He gave me a soft kiss on the forehead and I felt like I was in high school all over again, young and silly.

AJ and I went to a jazz performance in the park complete with a picnic from his favorite French Deli. That night we didn't talk about Erica, Leslie, Ric, or work. Just him, Josh and me.

That Sunday when Josh and I went to church with Libby I felt I had much to be thankful for and I told Libby so. While Josh was napping after church Libby and I talked about my date with AJ and what maybe next to follow. Libby was very happy for me but her common sense never took a day off, she told me to take my time with him and use my head not just my heart. She also told me to remember to pray and put God first. That's my Libby.

That Monday I was late for work, Erica acted as if she did not even see me come in. After I was seated she came over and said good morning, something about the glint in her eyes made me very uneasy. She was so nice it was positively sickening to watch. She told me how very sorry she was about Friday, that she was wrong for treating me that way and the things she had said about my son. Everyone in the office was listening and was just as shocked as I was. She also complimented me on my new outfit and that my hair looked wonderful, that she had no idea I had such a great head of hair.

I had begun to smell a rat with the apology now I knew something was wrong. After she finished her apologetic song and dance, she told me AJ was waiting to see me in his office.

When I got up to go to his office no one I passed would look me in the face. It was as if they knew something I didn't. I turned to see Erica perched on the corner of my desk smiling and looking like the cat that had swallowed the canary and just about to lick her paws at any minute. I continued toward AJ's office not wanting to look at anyone especially Erica. Then she came up behind me just as I reached for the doorknob and said you're getting just what you deserve. Before I could make a comment AJ opened the door and invited me in, he had a blank expression on his face that I could not read.

I walked in and he closed the door in her face before she could speak to him. But somehow even that could not change the sinking feeling that I had. He came to me and gave me a soft kiss and said good morning in a way I was not quite sure how to take.

He told me he had great news and a way to get Erica off my back. There was a chair behind me and I sort of fell into it. He did not notice but continued talking. He told that one of the other offices had an opening for an office manager trainee and he had recommended me for the position. He told me that this person was very happy to let me take the position because he had seen my work and contrary to Erica's opinion felt my work was very good.

I asked what gave him the idea for this stroke of genius, he told me he had spent Sunday afternoon with his mother and told her all about me and Josh. He said that his mother told him that it would be best to let me go to another office, of course he did not agree. But once she told him it would prevent another cat fight between Erica and me and would be complete rumor control he knew she was right. So he took her advice, talked to some of the other partners in the firm and found out that Geoffrey would be losing his office manager to her new baby in another month, so he spoke with him and things were set. Ms. Templeton would train me to take her place before she left on permanent maternity leave. I told him I did not want to work anywhere else, for anyone else. But he told me it was for the best because he would not have me treated badly by anyone especially Erica. He held me close and kissed me gently then whispered in my ear that we were expected at his parents' house for dinner that night. I told him that I couldn't possibly find a sitter on such short notice. He told me that Josh was expected also.

This made me uncomfortable because Josh did not take well to strangers and I told AJ of my concerns. He told me that he felt it was best for Josh to get to know his family because he felt that in the very near future Josh would be spending a great deal of time with them.

So much had been said that morning that I completely missed that last statement, the part about Josh being around them in the very near future escaped me altogether...for that moment.

As I was leaving AJ's office I noticed someone was packing my belongings in a box. He stopped as I approached and began to introduce himself to me. I neither heard nor cared about who he was. All I noticed was that he was holding my picture of Josh. I took my photograph and told him that I was perfectly capable of packing my own things. He told me he was one of the senior partners, one of which whose name was on my paycheck, and I began to instantly pay more attention.

Especially since everyone knew who he was except me. As had been the pattern of my entire morning thus far.

Geoffrey turned to AJ and told him that his choice in staff was improving greatly and gave a sharp glance in Erica's direction.

She suddenly noticed something very important on the floor beside her. But the anger on her face was very obvious. She stepped up beside AJ and he moved and she became even angrier, I thought steam was going to explode from her ears at any moment.

Erica's anger was not so much directed at these two men, but because she had been made a fool of. That morning when AJ told her that I was leaving, she was so busy gloating she did not hear him when he told her why. She just assumed that I was being terminated. Never in a million years did she think I would get a promotion, not to the office of a senior partner. A position she had wanted from day one. Hoping it would make AJ miss her and realize how much he needed her. And how good they would be together away from the office as well.

My packing was done and I was picking up my box to leave when AJ and Geoffrey both reached for it simultaneously. Geoffrey took the box and started toward the elevator. As I turned to tell everyone good-bye they all stood and clapped for me because they knew I had earned it the right way.

 AJ gave me a hug and told me he would miss my smiling face and then whispered in my ear, "until tonight anyway".

Geoffrey pushed for the elevator as I got near it almost dropping my box, I looked down to see that I was still holding my photo of Josh, my good luck charm.

CHAPTER NINETEEN.....
GEOFF'S GOOD LUCK

Geoff, as he liked to be called, told me on the elevator that he hoped I would like my new position. He said that he had seen some of my work and that he felt that I was perfect for the position. I felt on top of the world, yet I felt that I had lost something very important. Like a child leaving home for the first time.

Geoff and I got off on the sixth floor. He introduced me to the small group of people busing themselves around the office. He explained that these people were the ones that did most of the hard work.

Then this short dark haired lady came around the corner with a glass of milk. Geoff introduced me to Charlene Templeton, the woman I was to be trained by. That was obvious because they had told me she was leaving because she was having a baby and I could clearly see this lady was very pregnant. She was also very beautiful.

She came over and shook my hand, Geoff asked if he was needed anymore and she told him not at the moment. He welcomed me once again and then excused himself to his office.

Charlene showed me to an office right beside the one that Geoff had entered a few minutes before. It was wonderful and Charlene told me that this was my new office. She told me she had cleared out all her things so I could go ahead and move in. She told me she would be back in a few minutes, she left me alone I guess to get use to it.

The phone rang, it was AJ and he told me he missed me already. I began to unpack my things, as AJ and I spoke on the phone. I opened a drawer and found stationary with the company letterhead and my name on them, a gift from AJ. I suddenly became very excited about the whole thing and I could not wait to call Libby.

I sat there at the desk thinking to myself, I had a private office and my own secretary that just happened to be a guy. His name was Alexander. Alex seemed to take great pride in his job. There seemed to be something a little different about him but I was not quite sure what it was. Maybe it was just me. I came out and Alex introduced himself, he told me they would be coming to put my nameplate on the door.

He said it was supposed to be done before I got there but there had been a mix up and that he was truly sorry. I told him it was okay that it would be nice to watch. The men arrived and began working on the nameplate, it was very strange to see my name on the door, but it felt good.

Geoff came to see me and Charlene, I asked about Alex and Geoff told me that AJ had chosen him for me, he said if I didn't like him I could choose another secretary. I thought it was great that AJ was so concerned about me and I liked the feeling it gave me knowing he cared.

Alex tapped on the door, everyone looked at me and I said, "come in", and Alex entered with a cup of hot herbal tea and a saucer of lemons. That was it, Alex had won my heart. He said that everyone in the office drank coffee but Charlene and I were not allowed to, that we were ladies and had to drink tea (decaffeinated) tea. I agreed and we all had a laugh. Alex excused himself and told me to call if I needed him.

Charlene and I discussed how to use the call system with all the buttons that I had never seen on a phone before except in AJ's office and the switchboard office downstairs.

Charlene sat in the chair across the desk and began to explain my daily assignments, as I listened my mind started to wander. I began to think about what AJ had said earlier. Charlene saw the distant look in my eyes and she left closing the door behind her, leaving me to my thoughts.

CHAPTER TWENTY.....
JOSH GETS HIS WISH

I was thinking about that night and was very nervous. I was thinking about the conversation I had shared with Josh that past weekend and his words kept coming back to me. I guess my fear was that Josh would not like sharing his mommy with anyone, especially another man. I also began to think about the problem that I would have if Josh did not like AJ.

That evening when I picked up Josh from the daycare center I told him that I wanted him to meet AJ and that AJ and I were friends. I told Josh that AJ was a special person and that I hoped that he and AJ would be good friends. I explained that AJ would be coming over later to meet him and I wanted him to be on his best behavior and later we could talk about his feelings. I prayed that things would go well because I did care a lot for AJ but there would be a problem if Josh did not like him. I would not choose a man over my child, I knew that type of pain firsthand.

Sometimes I felt that I spent more time protecting Josh from life than encouraging him to live it. That night my fears were proved groundless, for Josh and AJ seemed to take to each other right away. They sat and talked while I got our coats. They acted as if they had known each other for years. AJ was as intrigued by Josh as Josh was him.

During our drive to AJ's parents' house they talked and I sat quietly and listened. At times I felt like an outsider. AJ would look over at me and wink then continue his conversation with Josh.

When we arrived they were discussing whether or not Josh was heavy. After opening my door, AJ lifted Josh and carried him in on his shoulders to prove to Josh that he was not heavy.

Mrs. Smith was more beautiful in person than her photo. All of her Indian heritage was glowing proudly, she thought Josh was a handsome little man and told him so. He began to blush and hide his face behind my coat. But I could tell he loved the attention. He was a little nervous but it did not last very long, for AJ's mother possessed that same ability to put people at ease very quickly and Josh was soon smiling and talking to her. At first he stood very close to me and held my hand, it made us both more comfortable. Then he moved away a little and I felt alone.

Mr. Smith entered the room and Josh and I both jumped a little. Josh had this look like he was debating whether to run or not. He reached for AJ's hand, partly because he was closest to him and partly because I was also holding AJ's hand; therefore, he couldn't get to mine. AJ was a mirror image of his father, except for the hair and the wrinkles.

He asked why it had taken AJ so long to come and visit, gave him a bear hug that would have shattered bones in anyone else. Josh took this opportunity to climb up on the couch out of the way. Mr. Smith looked down and saw Josh and something in his face changed, he sat near Josh on the couch and asked his name.

He spoke to Josh with the same gentleness his wife had used earlier and Josh responded in the same manner. It was as if Josh knew he was safe and he let it show.

I felt a tug on my hand and turned to see Mrs. Smith. We left the room and went to the sitting room. Mrs. Smith was very polite and it was a little uncomfortable at first. I could not tell if that was her way or if she was just being nice.

After we had talked for a few minutes I realized that she was just a very polite person and I was just paranoid. She told me to please call her Tatianna or Tia. It felt weird, but I agreed to try.

We sat and talked about men, children, jobs and families all the usual things that women talk about. During the conversation I learned a great deal about the man that I had become so fascinated with, as I'm sure his mother learned a lot about Josh and I. That he could be easily annoyed by things that others never paid attention too. Like his name, which he got from his father and grandfather, but had an issue with. For example, he was called "AJ" because although he loved and admired his father and grandfather he did not care for his middle name; and family and close friends called his father Giovanni so to close family he was Vanni and to friends and coworkers he was AJ. Talking to her was like talking to Libby. I got up to check on Josh and she told me not to worry so much that Josh was going to be fine. She told me of her conversations with Vanni, her pet name for AJ, I giggled a little and she realized that he had not told me, she made me promise not to tell him that I knew.

I peeked in on Josh, he and AJ wrestled on the floor while his father sat and watched them like a proud papa, coaching Josh along.

When Mrs. Smith and I entered the room Josh was telling them what he wanted to be when he grew up. Then Mr. Smith asked Josh if he knew what he wanted for Christmas, Josh said he wanted a baby brother or sister, and a special gift for me. I could tell by the look on his face that AJ was going to insist that Josh tell him. Josh said he wanted mommy to be happy with her new friend. AJ promised to make sure that mommy got Josh's special gift, he looked up at me and winked. His mother was still standing beside me and she gave my hand a little squeeze and a smile.

AJ told Josh that Santa really liked little people who thought of others with their Christmas wishes. This really impressed Josh that AJ knew so much about Santa.

Dinner was excellent, Josh had a chair right next to AJ's father. He seemed to belong there. Mr. Smith and Josh whispered and laughed all through dinner. It was interesting to watch and I became even more interested when I realized how AJ and his mom were also watching the happy pair.

After dinner we all sat around talking about this and that, of course Josh went to sleep. AJ was holding him in his lap and did not want his mother to put Josh down so he could sleep comfortably. His parents wanted Josh and I to stay overnight but I wanted to go home.

On the way home AJ was very quiet, I kept trying to get him to talk. He said he had a lot on his mind, I remained quiet the duration of the trip home.

The next day I called Libby to tell her about our trip to the Smiths'. I told her about Josh and AJ's parents. Libby and I laughed at the way Josh imitated AJ's father. Libby said that she always knew Josh would be smart as a whip. Libby loved us both dearly and she was a part of our lives that would forever be special. I promised Libby that I would bring AJ to see her. Two weeks later I did.

Those two weeks went by very quickly. We spent quite a bit of time together, he fell in love with Josh and Josh with him. I always seemed to get left out when those two got together, but it was wonderful to stand back and watch these two enjoy each other. AJ never came to visit without bringing Josh and me some type of gift. I tried to discourage this but, it was not going to happen. He had developed a great love for Josh and I and he never missed an opportunity to show it in every possible way. I began calling him Vanni as his mother and family did and at some point expected him to say something, instead he answered as he always had regardless of how I addressed him; as AJ or Vanni. It only made me feel closer to him to be allowed to use the name that only his mother had used.

The weekend I took Vanni to the ranch he was getting over a bad cold, Libby insisted that I bring him out so he could get some good home cooking. Vanni did not really feel up to visiting anyone but Libby would not take no for an answer. We spent the day and after Libby fixed Vanni one of her remedies for colds he was out like a light so, we spent the night and he woke the next morning feeling much better.

Libby warned us that once the news spread about us we would see changes in people.

We spent many more weekends at the ranch with Libby. Vanni and Libby got along beautifully, they became close friends and talked a lot even when I wasn't around. I was glad that they got along so well. Libby teased Vanni about having an old soul. He grew to love her as much as Josh and I did. He began bringing her gifts as he had with Josh and me.

CHAPTER TWENTY-ONE....
LETTING GO

When word finally got out that Vanni and I were dating, Erica quit her job. Not just working for Vanni but the firm as well. Libby told us that she felt that was the only reason Erica was working there anyway.

Two weeks after his divorce was finalized Vanni asked me to marry him, of course I said yes. Libby told me that she was glad that she was wrong about Vanni and me. Libby gave me a big hug and told me that she was glad that life was finally giving me what I deserved. I could only smile because I was trying to keep from crying because only Libby knew the pain I had suffered.

While Libby and I were discussing plans for the wedding the doorbell rang. It was Sky. He had gotten a letter from Libby about Vanni and me. Naturally he had to come to see if this man was all that Libby said he was.

He came in and saw me and grabbed me in a bear hug. He saw Josh and grabbed him up the same way. Even though my brother and I did not spend as much time together as we did when we were younger he was still very special to me and protective of me.

As we sat there catching up on Sky's work in Europe, Vanni came in. He did not know that Sky was going to be there and was very glad to finally meet him. They shook hands and Vanni tried to make conversation but Sky was kind of quiet. I think he felt he still needed to protect me.

They walked out to the stables, Libby had told Sky that he and AJ shared a love for horses.

They stood next to Blu a mare that I fell in love with when I graduated from college and was spending a lot of time at the ranch with Libby. Vanni was brushing Blu and did not seem to be saying much. Sky was doing most of the talking and that's what made me so nervous because Sky was very shy and never had a lot to say to anyone. Whatever he was saying was not affecting Vanni too much because he was still half-smiling. Josh was standing beside me in the window seat with a long face.

He was not happy about having to share his uncle with anyone, there were even times I was not invited in on their male conversations. I was afraid that Sky was would scare Vanni too much with his protective attitude which to some could be seen as just meanness, which was done out of love for Josh and me. Libby seemed to read my thoughts because she told me not to worry and put her arm around me. I put my head on Libby's shoulder and hoped that she was right.

That night on the porch swing Vanni got really quiet, I asked why he was keeping secrets. He told me I was the one keeping secrets. Unsure of his meaning I started to ask him what he meant but he continued on. He wanted to know why I had not told him about my past. I walked to the railing and over my shoulder I asked him what he meant. I had told him about Ricardo when we talked that morning in his office. He told me that Sky explained why he was so protective. I could not turn to face him because in his voice I could hear that he was referring to another part of my past that I had tried to bury forever. He said he was aware of how I grew up and about Charles. I felt my heart sink. There was something in his voice that made me feel cold and uncomfortable as I listened to him speak?

Vanni walked up behind me and put his face in my hair and asked why I had never told him about those things. I didn't have an answer because there wasn't one. He turned me to face him. He told me that I had suffered all the pain in this life that I was ever going to. He lifted my chin so I had to look in his eyes. He told me that he loved me and Josh and that he would make every effort to assure our happiness and safety.

The next day Sky and Josh took a horseback ride like always when Sky came to visit. I think it was meant to be a way for them to talk about Vanni and Josh's feelings without Vanni and I being there. That way Josh would speak freely something he always did with Sky. I should not have worried they came back laughing and covered in mud, I could not imagine how those two got into half the things they did.

Apparently they came across a young lady whose colt had gotten stuck in the mud while she was leading it and riding the mare. I was very surprised that they had run into anyone out here in the middle of nowhere. But Libby informed me that she had a neighbor that she had only glimpsed a few time through the trees.

The young woman's name was Amina Laurel. Something tickled the back of my mind but I could not have said why. I knew this woman was important but my mind would not hang on to anything and that thought would never come into focus.

Either way my brother and my son had to be gentlemen rescuers and gotten severely muddy in the process. But the colt was saved and Sky had come back with a twinkle in his eye that I had only ever seen once before. That had been a long time ago when we were children, also I had never told Sky that I noticed. I was informed by Libby as they were remanded to the outside showers that the tide had changed course and Sky's life was about to change. I think for a moment I felt jealous of having to share my brothers' attention with another woman. But at that very minute Vanni walked up and started rubbing his lips on my neck. This, he said helped him think better and distracted me from going to negative places in my mind. How right he was, I could not think at all.

I began to see the truth of Libby's words when a week later Sky said he wanted to stay around till the wedding instead of leaving and returning two weeks before the wedding. I was the only one that seemed surprised. I remember feeling as if my family was keeping secrets from me. But truth was I did not see what was happening with Sky and Amina because I did not want to see it.

Sharing was not ideal but if it kept Sky on the ranch with us, I was glad that Amina was living on the next ranch and was just as attracted to my brother as he was to her. The problem was what was Amina hiding or running from. Her fear was almost palpable when she was around. I tried very hard to be welcoming and nice to her but something was wrong and everyone knew, especially Sky.

I expected her fear to make Sky uncomfortable enough to back away, instead it brought out the protector I have always known my brother to be; I just never expected it to be in defense of someone other than me and I came face to face with the green-eyed monster that Sky was dealing with having to share me and Josh with Vanni. I made attempts to draw Mina (as Sky had started calling her) into conversations about herself, her family or just life in general. Nothing worked and it began to really bother me, Libby said to 'let sleeping dogs lie' because she felt like I was pushing too hard. I was never sure if I was asking questions simply to get to know her or if was looking for something to use to keep some distance between her and my beloved brother.

In the end I did as Libby said and found that to be more difficult than expected but, once Vanni agreed with Libby I had no choice. Especially when he mentioned the fact that I had difficulty sharing and revealing my own past. Leave it to my husband to be one that cut to the bone. I finally made peace with the jealous little sister in me and let the adult woman rule my actions.

CHAPTER TWENTY-TWO....
FAMILY LOVE

Libby and Mama Smith had begun working on wedding plans the same day that they met. I was expecting fireworks but they got along well. Libby and Aunt Alice made my gown and it was breathtaking.

I have a nervous habit of not eating when I am stressed or under pressure. AJ's mom and his aunt made sure I ate and stayed as relaxed as possible. I felt so comfortable with Vanni's family, it was like I had always been a part of them.

Josh had one day asked Mr. Smith what he was going to be to him, after Vanni and I were married, and he asked him what would he like for him to be. Josh confided that a few of friends had grandparents and he did not, but wanted them so Mr. Smith sat with Josh in his lap and explained that Josh now had grandparents and that in his mind Josh was his as much as Vanni was. Again he asked Josh what would he like to call him and Josh responded "babah". They had a good laugh about it and that was the end of it. Tatianna became Bella, Josh's version of "abuela", it means grandmother but I liked the sound of it so I started using it too. For me, Mr. Smith was just babah, not sure why but that is what Josh liked, so we both used that too. He loved it and thought it made him special because it was something Josh made up just for him.

My life had changed so drastically in a short amount of time and I was at times fearful that it was a beautiful dream that I would wake from to find myself waking in the middle of one of my parent's ugly fights. I knew this was irrational but when you grow up in a household like mine and Sky's it makes you not trust happy, pleasant and fun. Those terms were unfamiliar ground and you can't enjoy them because you know that there really is a monster, but it doesn't hide in the closet or under the bed. It walks around on two feet and sleeps down the hall.

When Vanni found me staring into space with a pained expression and a faraway stare, as he called it, he would nuzzle and kiss my neck and tell me to come back from that dark place because I was so far away that he missed me. I would always smile because strangely enough that is exactly how it felt when I came to myself.

Vanni and I discussed wedding plans and tried to come up with options that would satisfy us and calm the masses. The masses being the huge demands of Libby, Aunt Alice, his aunt and Bella. In the end it just could not be done, so Libby and Bella decided it was best if we choose what we would like and let that be.

When Vanni was younger he had always wanted a boat of his own that he could sail all by himself, so for his thirty-first birthday his father had given him a hundred-foot yacht. It was christened The Lafayette. So we were married at sea. My brother gave me away, after reminding AJ (my brother would not call him Vanni) that it was a loan. Josh was our ring bearer. Ashley consented to being my Matron-of-Honor. I expected resistance from her because we had never been close and the "Charles incident", as it was always referred to, did not help. But I suspect that she could not stand up to Libby and Bella once they got going. I had to enlist the help of Libby to acquire Amina as a bridesmaid, she was so shy. But it went off without a hitch.

My wedding brought my family together, something we had not been in a while. Mother and her new husband were there and she and Libby have become tolerable friends, meaning they tolerate each other and don't hesitate to use each other to accomplish a desired goal.

Surprisingly, my father sent a gift and his apologies for not attending, although no one expected him too and hoped he didn't. It would have been difficult for everyone.

Because Vanni was so well known everyone he knew was there or sent a gift. I remember telling him it would take longer to open all the wedding gifts than it would to get married. Vanni laughed because he thought so too. Babah was such a perfect father-in-law that I had a painting made from the photo of him on Vanni's bookshelf and he had it hung in their library, he loves it.

Josh asked if we could have a painting done and hung in his room, we promised to have it done right after the honeymoon.

Vanni expressed his desire to adopt Josh so that our family would be complete and I agreed. Gratefully Ric did not oppose the idea, he said it made sense because he had not spent very much time with Josh and Josh really did not know him anyway. He promised to write, then changed his mind as he realized there would be no point. We left it up to him as Vanni and I had no concerns about it affecting Josh negatively either way.

I remember the most special moment of the entire wedding took place when Libby caught me standing at the boat railing with tears in my eyes. She asked why the tears. I told her that once again she was right, life was finally giving me what I deserved. She gave me one of her motherly hugs that always made me feel loved. Just as she let go Vanni walked up and asked if he could have one of those. Libby kissed his cheek and thanked him for making her baby girl very happy. He smiled at Libby and held me very close as we watched the sun set on the water.

The sun setting at the close of one of the happiest days of my life, it seemed to be the close of so many things. My life as it had once been and Vanni's, too. It never ceases to amaze me how endings bring about so many beginnings. Once again I am at the end of a chapter in my life; but as always there is a new chapter beginning......

CHAPTER TWENTY-THREE.....
FULL CIRCLE

We now have four children. Sometimes I feel as if I have five. Vanni is spoiled and can be as big a baby as any one of the four we now have.

Our eldest together is a boy named Brandon Giovanni. Vanni was not thrilled with giving our son his name, I would have my way and because he loved me; he would let me. Then came our daughter. She is named after Libby, Olivia Nikol. The youngest is Gregory Armando his name a gift to my beloved father-in-law. He is very much the vibrant, quick witted personality of his name sake. Even if Vanni was initially hesitant to name him such, he happily agrees that our youngest is perfectly named.

Olivia was only a few months old when Libby passed and never really had an opportunity to get to know the loving spirit for which she was named, but reminds us all daily that Libby is still very much with us.

I'm grateful for having been with Libby when she died, sitting at her bedside. Vanni came to the hospital to be with us. One of my most precious moments was when Libby asked him to hold her hand. Then she reached for mine and placed my hand in his. She said it was time for her to go but she was leaving Sky, the children and me in good hands. She said Vanni would look after us as she had tried too, and that Amina would be the one to help Sky find some happiness. Libby also told me I mustn't pick at Mina like a scab on a wound that wanted to heal if I would just leave it be. I have never doubted Libby, but Sky's scars are deep and I often wonder if he will ever truly heal.

Because she had spent most of her time there on the ranch we wanted to bury her there so she would always be with us, but that meant contacting Charles which I could not do. Vanni said it would be best handled through our lawyers. While we were trying to determine the best and least painful way, we found some legal paperwork in the library safe that indicated the property was legally Libby's and had passed to me so there was no need to make that dreaded contact with Charles. Libby had saved me again. It made the loss of her even more painful. I remember Vanni holding me close and telling me the pain would ease in time, it was impossible to believe at the time that I could ever live with that much hurt inside me. Of course, like Libby he was right.

We make it a family event to clean off her grave and place fresh flowers there regularly.

I still drive out to the ranch some weekends, it still holds some pain for me but it also holds the best memories of my life. Our children love the ranch as much as I do, especially Josh. It seems to be the one place we can be together even though we are all doing something different.

I still go to Libby's room and sit. I think about the stories she would tell me when I was young. I sit in her favorite rocking chair and stare out the window and try to see the things she saw or maybe the way she saw them, either way I can still feel her with me. She is in every part of the house. Some days I can even smell food cooking when there is no one in the kitchen.

Vanni and the children insisted we keep Libby's room as she left it. It's almost as if they knew how much Libby meant to me, and they want to help me hold onto her wonderful memories.

Even though Libby is no longer with me she is in my heart and her words are always repeating in my mind. I felt blessed to have had her all those years when life was at its worst for Sky and me. She was always there when I needed her and sometimes I think she is still watching over us all.

Even now I am still not sure if Libby would have wanted me to write this book but Vanni says that Libby loved to tell her stories to others to help ease their pain. So I feel that this book will do just that.

The idea was Vanni's but the decision was mine. I decided to write it walking in the berry patch listening to Libby's headphones.

Because it was meant to be a part of our family forever. Sky lives at the ranch now. I think he's finally beginning to heal. To let go of the anger that has been so much a part of his life all these years.

Before I began writing this book I went to visit Sky so he could voice his opinion and his feelings. We walked in the berry patch and talked. He told me he felt that it was good to write the book. Maybe it would help someone else. He still does not let anyone get too close but at least now after seeing that all marriages are not like the one our parents had, he is considering giving love a try.

After discussing his feelings about the book we sat by the lake at the waterfall and watched the sun set over the lake beside the tree where our lives changed forever. Neither one of us could or wanted to say anything for fear of too many memories taking over. Memories that would surely bring the tears we promised never to cry again.

That weekend Sky and I spent it together and had those special talks we had as children that got us through all those years of pain and turmoil. I talked to Sky about opening up and letting someone love him the way Vanni loved me.

It was then that I learned many bridges had already been crossed as we walked in the berry patch. Sky told me that some things in his life had changed and he wanted to be sure before he said anything.

He told me about his feelings for Amina the young woman that had moved in the house on the other side of the lake. Sky had been spending time there helping her with repairs and trying to help her restore the place. He said it was during one of their afternoons painting that he caught Mina staring at him, so he asked what was so fascinating to her about him. Mina told him why she felt so comfortable with him and he so drawn to her was because they had known each other as children.

She reminded him of how we use to read to the children at St. Michaels Hospital and that she always waited for him and wanted no one else to read to her. He said it made him nervous and to buy himself some time to adjust, he asked her why just him? She told him, that he made her laugh changing his voice to sound more like the characters in the books, but more than that he made her feel special and safe. He asked her why that was so important and she told him it was because she had never felt that before.

Listening to him recall that afternoon with Mina and watching his face made me realize that Libby knew us so much better than we thought because she knew that Mina would be the one to help break the hold that our past had on my brother and that I would be forever grateful.

Mina was restoring the house and remodeling it, two things that Sky had a great passion for. Passions that I think were inherited from our mother but neither would admit if asked. Mina loved the house and all the work she and Sky had completed, they had worked on plans for the remainder of it because the house held a special place in her heart.

It had belonged to her grandfather. Sky told me that it was with her where he felt whole and happy. That he was hoping that they could have what Vanni and I had with each other. I could hear Libby's voice tell me to pray for it to be so and if it was good, God just may grant it.

I learned so much that day, so many things that had escaped me because planning and marrying a man like Vanni had taken my attention from almost everything except my son. I even took the month before the wedding off from work because I was stressed beyond distraction. Alex my assistant had finally told me to leave and not come back till after the wedding because I was making his job impossible. I remember we laughed about it often till I became pregnant with Brandon, then it started all over again.

Sky had told me about the shared love for rebuilding and restoring things that he had with Amina was what started the friendship, that and a colt stuck in the mud; but she alone was what made it grow into so much more. I know if one were to ask Mina she would say much the same about him. Sky admitted that my happiness with Vanni and the children had given him a new perspective. Mina was also trying to escape a painful past, knowing this gave Sky hope that he was not the only one still carrying pain from years gone by. I guess being with someone that knows your pain, or that can at least relate to it is therapy in itself.

I was hoping spending time with Mina would provide them both with whatever it was that they needed the most to live happily or at least close to it.

Our father died from a brain tumor no one knew he had except his doctor. A recent development or a long-term one, we will never know.

Father's will requested that he be cremated. I took care of the arrangements with help from Vanni. No one expected mother to attend but we looked for Sky, he did not come but a flower arrangement arrived unsigned, Mina I suspected as Sky would never have even considered it.

My mother was not comfortable with the writing of this book but she understood my need to write it. I was hoping she would read it and gain a better perspective of the child she thinks she lost to Libby.

I have returned to the berry patch to look at the fields, the waterfall and the lake. A thunderstorm has recently passed over and soaked everything. Although the ground is mud now, there is still a feeling that everything has been washed and is clean and fresh.

The storms always upset the children greatly for they fear the thunder and the lightning. But the storms no longer frighten me because I now know that all storms do end and that all clouds pass away in time.

I realize that my life will not be the same now that I no longer have Libby. But she gave me the continuing comfort of her love and her memories, she also taught me to pray and keep God at the forefront of our lives. Her giving me God and much love will be the things that keep her ever present in our lives and our hearts.

Libby taught me that God sends the rain from the storms to help things to grow and mature, in some cases it even helps life to gain strength. Vanni is my assurance from God that just as every cloud has a silver lining, after every storm there will be a rainbow.

For many years now I have felt Libby to be that rainbow. Vanni and the children are my pot of gold at the end. I pray that my brother finds his.

Enjoy an excerpt from the next storm tale

A Voice in the Rain

By

G. W. Duggan

What happens when someone you love dies? What happens to the time that you spent with them? What does your life become when the person that made you what you are leaves you? Questions will always arise; the problem is what happens when there is no one you trust to give you answers.

What happens when a stranger becomes everything to you, someone that does not have to love you but does anyway? Someone that fills up a void in your life that you never even knew existed. A person that makes you whole when you didn't even know you were in pieces. The person that gives you all the things that you are missing before you realize that they were not there; brings you all the things that were missing before you knew they were gone.

Libby was this person for me; she was mother, friend, guide, support, encouragement, resource, entertainment and protection. Simply, Libby was love.

Something I barely knew anything about, but desperately wanted. A force in my life to provide me with what every little girl needs and should never be without.

Libby brought so much into our lives that we were lacking, that we often wondered how we survived before she came. Yes along with Libby came Charles but, life must have balance; so there will always be some clouds in the sky even when we have the sun.

Libby was like the rain that falls from the clouds and washes everything and helps maintain and restore life. Charles was the thunder and lightning that reminds us to respect nature and never ignore the warning of a pending storm.

Although I find myself bereft without her presence, I can often times still hear Libby's voice speaking to me, encouraging me and guiding me. There times when the spring rains come to the ranch and I find myself standing at the edge of the porch railing looking out over the fields, those are the time when Libby's voice is strongest and loudest. Like the she is speaking to me from the falling rain, letting me know that she is ever with us and watching over us.

I often ask myself what would she tell me to do in this or that situation, what would her reaction be to something that's being said or done. Must I live on without her love and support, what will I do when I need answers and she is not here to provide them. Then the answer came to me, Vanni. Yes the wonderful man that came into my life at a time when I needed to be loved, appreciated and accepted with all my broken parts and cracked pieces. Turn to the beautiful gift that I was given as if in preparation for my loss of Libby. Even now I can still feel her presence as strongly as if she were right here beside me. A whisper on the wind, a voice in the rain.

To you the reader:

I hope that you enjoyed reading this book as much as I enjoyed writing it just for you. Know then that life will bring you much and often times not enough, but remember: "The rose does not have to bloom in your yard for you to enjoy its fragrance or its beauty and you are spared the pain of its thorns." Understand that just as a child often grows into what it sees and hears, be prepared to see the manifestation of your actions standing before you in the very near future. This means that not only do hits, punches and kicks cause physical damage, they cause emotional and psychological harm as well. So be aware that our children see and they learn. How to love when shown love, how to hate when shown hate and how to hurt when they have been shown hurt.

Special Thanks To ...

To my Father in heaven, for all that He is and all that He is not. Thank you for Grace and Mercy; love and peace; joy and pain. For each one shapes us, molds us and helps to create Gods most perfect work.

To everyone who taught me valuable lessons. My "Mommy" who has been an inspiration and a guiding force in my life. To JA for all that you are and all that you help me become. To RW for helping me learn the joy of forgiveness. My best friend KW, who could very well be the "Vanni" for the right woman. My own children, they know who they are. To MKD who taught me that things are not always what they seem. To the one who taught me how to love, and how to let go, blessings MAG. To my friend STW, life would not have been the same without you. I will always love you and thank God for you. To my "lil sister" Tay, there is no way to say what you mean to me, but I have the assurance of knowing that you know. To my buddy 7 years, you already know. To my sister, who is also my prayer partner and very best friend; I give thanks for you daily to God for giving me a "Sky" in you. To MOD & B, all I can say is that I will forever love you and carry you in my heart. Thanks to CA for being one of the Libby's in my life. To my CSD thank you for believing in me and helping me on the road to getting it done. I will always remember "new level, new devil". To the ladies of Esther, God has a special place in heaven for all of you and I pray we all meet there one day. To both my grandfathers there will never again be men like you.

PGMF & MBCF, there are simply no words except, Thank you.